# DARK TIDE

## Soliloquy Titles by Greg Herren

Sleeping Angel

Sara

Timothy

Lake Thirteen

Dark Tide

# DARK TIDE

*by*

## Greg Herren

2014

ISBN 13: 978-1-62639-197-0

This Trade Paperback Original Is Published By
Bold Strokes Books, Inc.
P.O. Box 249
Valley Falls, NY 12185

First Edition: September 2014

---

**Credits**
Editor: Ruth Sternglantz
Production Design: Susan Ramundo
Cover Design By Sheri (graphicartist2020@hotmail.com)

# Acknowledgments

I am without doubt the luckiest author alive. I live in the city I love with the man I love doing the work I love, and none of it would be possible without the generosity and kindness of a lot of wonderful people.

I'm incredibly lucky to have as my day job the NO/AIDS Task Force. I work with a group of people who always make me laugh, can always put a smile on my face, and always keep me grounded. From our amazing department head J. M. Redmann to my direct supervisor Josh Fegley to my co-workers at the Community Awareness Network office, they make going to work a great joy for me. So thanks to Drew Davenport, Joey Olsen, Tiffany Medlock, Augustin Correro, Alex Leigh, Jeremy Beckford, Mark Smith, and Nick Parr for all you guys do. Gone on to other jobs but never to be forgotten are Martin Strickland, Allison Vertovec, Robin Pearce, Brandon Benson, Matt Valletta, Larry Stillings, Sarah Ramteke, and Tanner Menard—miss you guys. And of course, the Evil Mark—Mark Drake—who occasionally still comes by on Fridays and always brings that cold chill with him.

Working with Bold Strokes Books has been an enriching and enjoyable experience from the moment I signed my first contract. The support staff and the community of writers Radclyffe has assembled is extraordinary and special, and I couldn't be prouder to be a part of it. Special recognition is due my two editors, Ruth Sternglantz and Stacia Seaman. I also need to thank Sandy Lowe for all of her able assistance with all kinds of things, Cindy Cresap for putting up with my utter inability to ever know what book she needs more information from me about, the cover designers who have given me exceptional covers that take my breath away, and everyone else there I've worked with—too many to try to remember because I know that I will forget someone. Thanks, Radclyffe, for letting me be a part of this.

I have the most extraordinary friends, who are always there to cheer me on when I don't want to write another word. Special thanks to Susan Larson, Pat Brady, Michael Ledet, Jesse and Laura Ledet, Bev and Butch Marshall, Stan and Janet Duval, Karissa Kary, Konstantin Smorodnikov, 'Nathan Burgoine, Timothy J. Lambert, Becky Cochrane, Billy Martin, Ked Dixon, Rob Byrnes, Michael Thomas Ford, Wendy Corsi Staub, Lisa Morton, Vince Liaguno, Victoria A. Brownworth, Carol Rosenfeld, Amie M. Evans, Pat King, Michael Carruth, John Angelico, Harriet Campbell Young, Mark Richards, Sally Anderson, Stephen Driscoll, Stuart Wamsley, Marc Scharphorn, and so many, many others I cannot even begin to name them all.

A huge shout out to the awesome Beth Hettinger Tindall for doing such a great job on my website!

Everyone on Facebook—thanks for making me laugh and distracting me when I need distraction!

The FL's—what can I say? You make me laugh till I cry, you enable me, you instigate, and you never let me forget that I'm white trash, quite frankly, or that maybe I just need to take a Xanax. You're always there whenever I need you, and you make me happier than you could ever possibly know. And at least I know when you're talking about me behind my back, you're checking out my great ass. It takes a village.

And of course, the love of my life and my reason for getting out of bed every morning: Paul Willis. Thank you for everything.

## Dedication

This is for Ruth Sternglantz, a great friend
and an even greater editor

## CHAPTER ONE

The engine of my pickup truck made a weird coughing noise just as I came around a curve in the highway on the Alabama Gulf Coast and I saw Mermaid Inn for the first time.

My heart sank.

*That's not good,* I thought, gritting my teeth. I looked down at the control panel. None of the dummy lights had come on. I still had about a half tank of gas. I switched off the air conditioning and the stereo. I turned into the long sloping parking lot of the Inn, pulling into the first parking spot. I listened to the engine. Nothing odd. It was now running smooth like it had the entire drive down. I shut the car off and kept listening. There was nothing but the tick of the engine as it started cooling.

*Maybe I just imagined it.*

Hope springs eternal.

I took a deep breath while sitting there, listening closely to make sure.

The last thing I needed was to spend money on getting the stupid old truck fixed. Maybe it just needed a tune-up. I couldn't remember the last time it had one.

Dad gave me the truck when I turned sixteen. It had been his work truck since before I was born—it was two years older than I was. He'd finally broken down and bought himself a new one. This old one was dependable and had almost two hundred thousand miles on it. Dad had taken good care of it. He'd babied it, gotten an oil change every three thousand miles without fail, and I could count on one hand the number of times it had been in the shop to be repaired. It still had the original transmission.

It might not have been the nicest or prettiest car in my high school parking lot, but it got me where I needed to go and got good gas mileage. Since I was saving every cent I could for college, that was a lot more important than horsepower and cosmetics and a loud stereo that rattled your back teeth. The swimming scholarship I'd accepted from the University of Alabama wasn't going to remotely cover anything close to the lowest estimate of what my expenses might be, but it was the best offer I'd gotten.

And I was grateful to have it. If they hadn't offered, I wouldn't be going at all.

Swimming was my ticket out of Corinth, Alabama.

My only other option was to go work for my dad's business, and I didn't want to clean pools or do landscaping for the rest of my life.

Dad didn't want me to, either.

So I needed to save as much money as I could. I worked part time at the Hardee's and worked for Dad. I packed lunch every day instead of buying lunch at Corinth High. I wore my clothes until they were rags. I ignored the other kids who made fun of me for shopping at the Tuscaloosa Goodwill. I didn't go to prom. I didn't date. I didn't buy yearbooks or a letter sweater or a class ring. I saved change and rolled it to take to the bank.

Dad would help me out as much as he could, but I didn't want him making any more sacrifices for me than he already had. He wasn't exactly rolling in cash. Years of paying for me to go to swimming camps had stretched his budget about as far as it could go.

*It's an investment,* he would always say, finding the money somewhere every summer. *If it gets you a scholarship, it's worth it.* Then he would always look sad. *I wish I could have afforded a coach. Maybe you could have gone to the Olympics...*

I resisted the urge to bang my head on the steering wheel.

Maybe it was nothing. Maybe some air just got in the fuel line or something.

It needed to be checked out anyway. Dad always said it was better to get it checked out when it could be fixed cheaply rather than later when it would cost an arm and a leg.

Hopefully I wouldn't have to dip into my college fund.

I took a deep breath. Nothing to be gained by wasting energy worrying about it.

It was what it was.

I wiped sweat off my forehead with the tail of my shirt.

The windows of the old Nissan pickup weren't tinted. The hot June sun was turning the interior of the cab into an oven. I unfolded the reflective sunshade stored behind the driver's seat, pushing it up against the windshield, flipping the sun visors down to hold it in place. I opened the door and stepped out onto the hot asphalt. I stretched, feeling my lower back crack a bit.

I'd been driving for almost five hours, stopping only once for gas and to get something to eat just north of Birmingham. My stomach growled. I'd gotten hungry again about an hour north of Mobile but resisted the urge to stop. I'd eaten a protein bar, figuring it was better to get the damned drive over with. There were bound to be places to eat in Latona.

I grabbed my backpack from the passenger seat and pulled out my cell phone. I sent Dad a quick text letting him know I'd gotten here safely. No need to worry him about the truck until I knew more, I figured. I slid my arms through the straps of the backpack and shrugged it into place on my back. I glanced at my big duffel bag and the battered second-hand suitcase I'd found at a flea market. Both were heavy—maybe I should start the truck and pull up closer to the Inn? No, probably best to wait, I decided, locking the door and clipping my keys to a belt loop of my shorts. *Let it sit for a while, maybe whatever's wrong is just overheating or something.*

Wishful thinking never hurts.

I started walking up the long, sloping parking lot. The humidity hung over me like a wool blanket taken out of the dryer twenty minutes too soon.

I could feel the heat from the blacktop through the soles of my tennis shoes. Waves of heat shimmered up in front of me. After a few steps my socks were soaked through with sweat. Water was running down my scalp and my armpits. My cotton shirt adhered to my skin. The sun was high in a cloudless blue sky. There was only the slightest breeze blowing from the direction of the bay.

The blacktop was wide, with yellow lines marking out parking spaces on either side of a center aisle wide enough for two cars to pass side by side. At the top of the slope the paved surface leveled off in front of the Inn. There were about twenty or so parking spots, but only one other car in the lot. It was a dark green Subaru Forester, parked in the spot closest to the building. Beyond the paved surface on each side was white, powdery sand. Even with my sunglasses on the reflection of the sun on it was almost blinding. Sea oats and other tall grasses waved in the slight breeze coming in off the water.

I could barely see the water of the bay in the distance, over the high dunes on the other side of the enormous Victorian structure. A weathered wooden walk, raised high on gray wooden posts, led from the side veranda of the Inn through the dunes to the beach. The water in the distance glittered sapphire blue. Whitecaps, looking like half-moons, appeared and disappeared just as suddenly. I could see a sailboat so far in the distance it looked tiny. Farther beyond was the opposite shore of the bay, a barely visible line of green trees.

I could feel the sweat from my armpits running down my sides as I trudged along. I was thirsty, dehydrated. I'd finished the big bottle of water I'd brought with me just as I passed through Mobile. *Should have stopped and gotten another one,* I berated myself.

It felt like every drop of water in my body was coming out through my pores. My stomach growled again, and I gritted my teeth.

I started walking again.

*This parking lot should be full, shouldn't it? You'd think there wouldn't be a vacant room on the Gulf Coast in June,* I thought when I was about halfway up the slight slope.

I wiped my forehead with the tail of my shirt again. I could hear waves lapping at the shore behind the Inn. Gulls cried as they circled overhead, looking for food. A car passed on the road behind me, with some Beyoncé song blaring out the windows so loud the bass made my back teeth rattle. Just as suddenly it was gone, and besides the gulls and the waves everything was silent again.

It was eerie. There was no sign of life anywhere in the huge old Victorian house.

The Inn had looked impressive on the website. Those pictures online made it look like an enormous, multistoried mansion that was just a little weathered. In real life it looked even bigger but far less friendly and welcoming. The enormous dark windows looked ominous, despite the bright sunshine. Goose bumps come up on my arms. *It looks haunted,* I thought before shaking my head at my own stupidity.

There's no such thing as ghosts.

Or mermaids, for that matter.

The history tab on the website had said Mermaid Inn was a turn-of-the-century Victorian mansion originally built as the home of the Rossitter family. The Rossitters had owned a fleet of fishing boats pretty much responsible for the economy of the nearby town of Latona, Alabama, for many decades. It didn't say what had happened to the Rossitters—the page just said that the house had weathered numerous hurricanes and had stood empty for decades after World War II. It implied the Rossitters died out during the war. It went on to say someone named Jim Hampton had bought the place in the early 1970s. There had been extensive renovations done that had taken several years before it opened as an inn in 1974.

The man who'd hired me as the summer lifeguard was named Joe Hampton. He was probably Jim's son. He'd seemed nice when we'd talked on the phone yesterday. I'd applied for the job earlier in the spring, but Joe had hired someone else. Apparently, the guy he'd hired had changed his mind. I didn't mind being second choice or a last-minute replacement. The money was good, and it got me out of Corinth for the summer. I didn't mind working for my dad, but I knew life was about seizing opportunities.

I started walking again.

Mermaid Inn was painted a deep fuchsia color—the same shade as the blossoms of the four-o'clocks planted by my mother in the flowerbeds back home. Each window had a pair of shutters painted black. The shutters were open but the place still seemed closed off. There was a gallery running around the entire first floor, and a partial gallery on the second. The rooms on the third floor had balconies. The sloped black roofline was interrupted here and there by the occasional gable, which almost seemed like hooded eyes. I took a deep breath. It almost felt like the place was watching me.

*You're being silly,* I chided myself. *It's just a big old house. This is about the nightmare you had last night.*

After we'd talked on the phone and I'd said yes, I'd had to pack hurriedly and explain everything to my father. Dad wasn't happy about it, but he'd accepted it as my decision. After I finished packing everything, I'd looked up Mermaid Inn's website again. I'd gone to bed earlier and been tormented by bad dreams all night—which was why I'd finally given up and gotten up so early. One dream had been about mermaids and mermen in the water, with sharp teeth and claws for hands. In another I was running through the halls of Mermaid Inn being chased by something—I didn't know what it was, but it wanted to kill me. It had been dark, a thunderstorm raging outside, as I climbed stair after stair, climbing up until there was nowhere to go except out onto the roof in the storm.

And once I was out there, with the wind and the rain lashing at me, I was trapped.

That was when I woke up.

*Just a dream. Get a grip, Ricky.*

It was just a big old house.

I started walking again.

According to the e-mail Joe Hampton had sent last night, my room was up on the fourth floor. He'd said my room was really *a little studio apartment, with full bathroom and a kitchenette, perfect for a single young guy.* The central air conditioning didn't go up to the fourth floor, so I'd have to make do with a window unit.

That didn't bother me at all. We didn't have central air back home, either.

I mopped the sweat off my face again as I climbed the steps up to the gallery. The front door was made of a dark, stained wood. A stained-glass window took up most of the top half of it. The stained glass depicted a mermaid sitting on the shore as waves came in around her. She was facing me, a knowing smile on her dark red lips. Her scaled green fish tail curled around her. She had bright red hair that hung down past her waist. One of her hands was extended in a beckoning gesture in front of her. The fingernails on that hand were long and painted red—and looked sharp. She looked...predatory.

*Just like in my dream.*

Goose bumps came up on my bare arms.

*You're being an idiot.*

I bit my lower lip. I reached for the knob and opened the front door. I stepped inside and closed the door. It was much darker inside and my eyes needed to adjust. It was also about thirty degrees cooler. The sudden change in temperature made goose bumps pop up on my skin. Again. I stood there shivering until my eyes finished adjusting.

I wiped my face dry with my damp shirt one last time.

A long hallway ran to the rear of the house. I could see another door at the far end. It matched the front door, with the same stained-glass mermaid design on the upper half. The sunlight streaming through it cast beautifully colored shadows on the floor. The floor was a dark hardwood, polished till it shone. A carpeted hanging staircase about midway down the hall led to the second floor. The banisters were carved from the same type of wood as the floor and glistened in the light. There were several shut doors along the hallway. A metal stanchion holding a sign with the word *Registration* written in it with a black Sharpie was just ahead on the right. At the top of the sign was an arrow pointing toward an open door.

I walked down the hall and stood in the doorway.

Seated at a wide desk in the back of the room was a teenaged girl. She looked to be about my age, give or take a year or so. Her skin was tanned a dark golden brown. The pale green T-shirt she was wearing had *Mermaid Inn* written in white script across the front above the same image from the stained-glass windows on the doors. She was using a calculator, a pencil clamped between her teeth. Her eyebrows were knit together in fierce concentration. She was scowling as she peered at the calculator, and then turned to an open laptop. She shook her head slightly and started typing away on the laptop keyboard. Her fingertips lightly brushed the keys so they didn't make a sound. She was so lost in what she was doing she didn't notice me standing in the doorway.

I cleared my throat and she looked up, annoyance written all over her face.

She forced a strained smile. "Hi, may I help you? Do you have a reservation?"

The smile didn't quite reach her hazel eyes. Her voice sounded canned and phony. I recognized the tone. It was the *I don't want to be bothered but have to be nice* tone of the put-upon service worker. I'd used it several times myself at Hardee's. She would be pretty if she ever actually really smiled, I decided. She had a pert little snub nose over a mouth that was maybe just a little too wide. Her teeth were even and white in her tanned, heart-shaped face. The corners of her eyes turned up slightly. There were slight indents in her cheeks that probably turned into dimples when she smiled for real. Her light brown hair had blond streaks in it, and it was pulled off her face in a tight ponytail that bounced when she moved her head.

"I'm sorry to bother you. My name's Ricky Hackworth, and—"

"You're the new lifeguard." She cut me off. Her tone was flat and cold. The phony smile faded. Her hazel eyes moved up and down quickly as she looked me over. A strange expression I couldn't read flashed over her face before she let out a long-suffering sigh. "We weren't expecting you until tomorrow. I haven't had a chance to even glance into your room yet." Her forehead wrinkled and she leaned back in her chair.

"Well, I spoke with Mr. Hampton yesterday, and he said arriving today wouldn't be a problem," I replied defensively. "I mean, I figured driving down on a Thursday would be easier than a Friday with all the weekend traffic, and having an extra day before I actually had to start work would give me a chance to get settled first. I drove all the way down from—"

"Yes, yes, I get it. But that isn't the point." She interrupted me again with a sideways shake of her head that sent the ponytail bouncing. "The point is Uncle Joe didn't tell me and your room isn't ready. And I don't have time to get it ready right now." She chewed on her bottom lip.

"I can do it myself. I don't want to be any trouble."

"Well, you're going to have to. Sorry, but I have to get these accounts straightened out today…" Her voice trailed off as she stared at the laptop screen. She pushed the chair back and stood up. She was barely five feet tall. She tilted her head back and raised her eyebrows. "Didn't you bring anything with you? All you have is that backpack?" The corners of her mouth went up a bit, like she wanted to laugh at me but was just barely managing to control herself.

"It's in my truck. I left it there—"

"Well, go and get your stuff." She tapped her foot impatiently. "Uncle Joe drove up to Mobile this morning and of course he isn't back yet. Like I said, I've got to get these accounts finished by this afternoon. I don't have all day." *Tap, tap, tap* with her sneaker-clad right foot on the hardwood floor. "You're burning daylight. I don't have all day."

*Uncle Joe.* When I'd talked to him on the phone, he'd mentioned a niece. His voice sounded so young I'd just assumed she was a small child. "You must be Cecily."

She didn't stop tapping her foot. "Yeah, I am. Nice to meet you," she said sourly. "And I wasn't kidding about hurrying."

"Could I get some water first?" I tried a smile on her, but it didn't work. "It's pretty hot outside, and I parked at the bottom of the lot—"

She rolled her eyes. "That wasn't very smart, was it?" She made a face. "Wait here." She walked past me to the doorway, where she paused. "As long as we don't have guests, you can park as close as you can. But when we have guests, *then* you park at the bottom." And then she was gone.

While I waited for her to come back, I looked around the room. The walls were painted beige, and the floor was polished hardwood like the hallway. Her desk sat on a faded Oriental rug that extended to the credenza behind and out to the center of the room. The curtains were closed on the french doors behind her desk, but I walked around it and peeked through them. From the window I could see the dunes stretching out to where the pine forest came down right to the bay's shoreline.

It seemed nice…but a bit off. I couldn't put my finger on what it was…then shook my head. *It's not like you've ever been in a hotel before,* I reminded myself. *And it beats the dorms at swim camp.*

I heard her footsteps coming back and hurried around to the front of the desk. She walked in and handed me a sweating bottle of water. I smiled my thanks to her and took a big swig.

It was delicious.

"So that's your blue truck parked out there?" she asked as she sat back down behind the desk.

I took another swallow and recapped the bottle. "Yeah."

"You drove that thing all the way down here from north Alabama? You're braver than I am." She gave me a nasty smile.

"It's a good truck, dependable." I said, remembering the weird coughing noise. "I do want to get something checked out, though. Is there a garage nearby?"

"Rocky's Auto Repair. Just follow the highway into town. It's on the left. You can't miss it."

"Thanks. I'll run the truck over there after I get settled."

"Glad I could help." She waved her hand. "Well, get your stuff. I don't have all day." She started pounding away at the laptop again.

I finished the water by the time I reached my truck. I climbed in and started it. The ignition caught and I revved the engine a few times. It didn't make the coughing noise again. But when I shifted it back into drive after backing out of the spot, the transmission seemed a little sluggish.

*Yeah, probably needs new spark plugs,* I told myself as I pulled into the closest spot to the front steps. *I hope that's all it needs.*

I grabbed my duffel bag and suitcase and lugged them into the Inn. She was waiting for me at the foot of the staircase. I followed her up. About halfway up to the second floor, the stairs gave slightly under my feet. I froze, unable to move as my mind flashed back to my dream. I could feel the slight edges of the terror creeping back into my head. *The stairs gave under my feet in the dream,* flashed through my head as I stood there, paralyzed, unable to move. *It's behind me, it wants to kill me...I've got to get out of here...*

My heart started racing.

With every ounce of my willpower, I turned my head and looked back.

Of course, there was nothing there.

"Are you coming?" she called impatiently from the top of the stairs. "I don't have all day."

*Drama queen,* I berated myself as I started climbing again.

When we reached the third floor she turned to the right. She walked past many closed doors with slightly tarnished brass numbers on them. At the end of the long hallway, she unlocked another door, which opened to a narrow staircase. "Your apartment is in the attic—the door with a *3* on it," she said, pulling out a small key ring from her shorts pocket and handing it to me. "The silver key is to your apartment, the brass key fits the front and back door locks as well as the door to this staircase. We always keep this door locked."

"Oh?"

She gave me a crooked smile. "Can't have the ghosts in the attic getting out and bothering the guests now, can we?" When I goggled at her, she stepped aside with an impatient shake of her head. "We keep it locked because we live up there. Sheesh."

"Oh yeah, of course."

She rolled her eyes, clearly thinking *what an idiot.* "Your apartment is to the right, first door. I'll send Uncle Joe up when he gets back. I'll get you some linens for your bed and bathroom."

Without another word she walked away.

There was no way I could make it up the narrow and steep staircase with both bags, so I heaved the duffel bag over my shoulder and climbed up. Once the door closed behind me, I started sweating again. It was like stepping into an oven. Some of the steps groaned under my weight as I climbed up. The hallway at the top was even hotter. I dumped my duffel bag on the hardwood floor and went back for my suitcase. I was drenched in sweat by the time I got it up to the short and narrow hallway. A big bay window looking out at the Gulf water was at the far end. I glanced out for a moment before fitting my key into the door on the right. There was another door farther down the hall with a brass *2* on it. The only door to the left had a *1* on it. The key turned easily in the lock. I swung the door open and gasped in relief as cold air washed over me. I stepped into a large room. The ceiling slanted down as it approached the far wall, leaving about three feet or so of clearance over the brass bed. I tossed my duffel bag and suitcase onto the bed and took a look around.

The room was sparsely furnished. There was an old avocado-colored Formica kitchen table with legs spotted with rust with two matching chairs. A battered and saggy-looking sofa was pushed up against one wall. A stained and scarred coffee table sat in front of the sofa. The ceiling slanted, and the bed was shoved up against the wall where the gable interrupted the slant. An empty bookcase stood against one wall. An ancient-looking television sat on top of a peeling faux-wood cart. The remote sat on the coffee table, next to an enormous mermaid-shaped ashtray. The kitchenette was just inside the door, on the left. There was a small rust-stained porcelain sink, an ancient-looking refrigerator, a small counter space underneath two cabinets, and a tiny microwave. There was also a cheap coffeemaker. The air conditioner mounted in the kitchenette window was blasting out cold air, but it wasn't nearly as cool up here as it had been on the lower floors.

But after the hell of the hallway, it felt fantastic.

I sat on the bed and sighed. It was nicer than some of the apartments I'd looked at online to get an idea of what I might be able to afford when school started that fall. *Home, sweet home,* I thought as I looked out the window in the gable. Over the tops of the sand dunes that separated the beach from the Inn, I could see the green shallows with the deeper blue water just beyond. The sailboat I'd seen earlier was nowhere in sight. The entire bay was empty as far as I could see in each direction. I knew the town was to my left, on a more inland curve of the shore near where a bayou emptied in the bay. Some gulls were perched on the storm gutter at the edge of the roof, and by looking straight down I could see the boardwalk across the dunes to the beach itself. The glare of the sun on the white sand was too intense to look at for long, but I noticed the beach itself was completely deserted.

*Why is this place not booked solid?* I asked myself again. *School is out, and even if it weren't, there are plenty of people without kids! There's a private beach and the bay is gorgeous. Maybe because Latona is such a little town and there's nothing to do at night?*

But other small coastal towns were jammed full of tourists in the summer. Why not Latona?

I opened the closet door and pulled the light string. A couple of rusty wire hangers dangled from the pole. There was also a slightly musty smell. *Put air freshener on grocery list,* I reminded myself, leaving the door open so it could air out.

I opened my backpack and set up my laptop on the Formica table. The tabletop was worn, with the occasional coffee stain and more than a few cigarette burns. My laptop found an open wireless network called *Mermaid Inn,* and I clicked on it to connect. I plugged my phone into a wall socket in the kitchenette and was about to set it down when I noticed a text: *Glad you made it safely. Be careful. Call if you need anything.*

*Thanks, I will,* I texted back.

The refrigerator was empty, as was the freezer. One of the cabinets in the kitchenette had a collection of cheap cups, glasses, some plates, and some battered pots and pans. The bathroom was hotter than the rest of the little studio, and there was a chipped porcelain claw-foot bathtub with a shower curtain on a rod hanging from the ceiling. I flushed the toilet and checked the sink to make sure there was hot water. There was another little closet in the bathroom containing threadbare towels and washcloths.

I was unpacking my duffel bag when there was a knock on my door.

It was Cecily. She was carrying a laundry basket filled with bed linens. She brushed past me without a word and set the basket on top of the bed. "Laundry room is on the first floor," she said, folding her arms and shifting her weight from one foot to the other as she spoke. "You're welcome to use it whenever you need it as long as we're not doing guest linens and stuff. You get paid every Friday." She frowned. "Like I said, if you want to go into town, you turn right onto Shore Road, and it goes right into town, it's the main street. There's a Piggly Wiggly and an Albertsons, gas stations, some fast-food places and markets and stuff, if you want to explore a bit. If you want to take your truck to Rocky's, it's on the main drag just past the Piggly Wiggly. They have a big sign, it's hard to miss." She took a deep breath. "I don't know what Uncle Joe told you about the job, but your days off are Tuesdays and Wednesdays—those are the days we're more empty than full—and town ordinance only requires us to have a lifeguard from ten in the morning until six at night. Other than your lunch break or going to the bathroom, you're expected to be on your tower from ten to six, Thursday through Monday. Our beach is technically private, but anyone can access it and we can't legally throw anyone off it." She rolled her eyes. "Your job is to make sure no one drowns."

"I'll keep that in mind," I replied sarcastically.

She made a face. "Having a lifeguard is a stupid expense, but we don't have a choice. Ever since those kids drowned a couple of years ago and they passed that stupid ordinance—" She cut herself off. "Anyway, if you have any questions about anything, let me know." Her tone made it clear she would prefer I didn't ask her anything. She paused at the door. "Uncle Joe and I also live on this floor. So try to keep the noise down." She looked up at me. "I don't know when Uncle Joe'll be back—he should be back already." She shrugged. "But he's going to want to talk to you at some point."

"And I can trust Rocky's not to try to rip me off?"

She closed her eyes and exhaled. "It's where Uncle Joe takes our cars to be serviced or when they need work. He trusts them, so just tell them I sent you." A smile briefly flashed across her face. "What kind of trouble are you having with your truck?"

I shrugged. "Made a funny coughing sound when I got here. Want to get it checked out."

"Yeah, well, that's probably a good idea." She started to close the door behind her but stopped. She turned back to face me and took a deep breath. "Look, I'm probably coming across like a bitch, and if I am, I'm sorry. Uncle Joe didn't tell me you'd be here today and you caught me off guard, okay? And I really do have a lot of work to do." She gave me a weak smile. "You seem like a nice enough guy."

I smiled back at her. "I like to think I'm a nice guy."

"Yeah, well." She started to close the door again but hesitated. She looked like she couldn't make up her mind whether or not to say something.

"Was there something else?"

"Just be careful, okay?" She exhaled.

"Careful?" I frowned. "What do you mean?"

"I mean we don't seem to have much luck with lifeguards," she replied, pulling the door closed shut behind her.

## Chapter Two

The truck started right up. I didn't hear any strange noises as I revved the engine. I backed out of the parking space and made a U-turn. As I put it into drive and accelerated, there was a bit of a hesitation before the car started moving. It was so sluggish I even double-checked to make sure I had it in the right gear. I mentally crossed my fingers that it wouldn't be anything too serious.

Or really expensive.

I turned right onto the shore highway. About fifty yards away the beach seemed to almost climb up onto the road. The dunes started sloping upward just beyond the solid white line. White sand was scattered all over the blacktop. I passed a few empty places where cars could park and access the beach. The white sands were deserted. Sea oats waved forlornly atop the dunes. Again I wondered where the vacationers and sunbathers were. And even if Latona wasn't much of a tourist destination, an undiscovered stretch of pristine beaches on the Gulf Coast, where were the locals?

Granted, Mermaid Bay was just an inlet off Mobile Bay. But it was still white sand beach and clear salt water. The other side of the road was a forest of towering pines, with bushes and brush gathered around the roots of the trees. About another hundred yards later the road curved away from the beach and went back into the pine forest. Spanish moss hung from massive live oaks like the beards of long-dead Confederate generals.

It was too hot to leave the air conditioning off. I rolled up the window and turned it on. I passed a couple of roads on the left side leading back into the forest. The city limit sign was maybe about another half mile after the first curve.

LATONA CITY LIMIT—POPULATION 23,475.

The sign was riddled with bullet holes.

Just past the sign, the road curved back toward the shore. Before long the road was running along the shoreline again. The trees gave way on either side to pavement. KFC, Burger King, McDonald's, Pizza Hut, Applebee's—lined up like obedient soldiers on the left side of the road. On the right there was a stone wall about three feet high. On its other side was the bay. Piers and sailboats and fishing boats and little marinas. There were signs of life now. Cars passing in the other direction. Other cars pulling out and driving the same way I was going. People of all ages and shapes and sizes on the sidewalks, getting into and out of cars, walking their dogs, and stopping to chat with friends. An occasional massive live oak dripping Spanish moss from enormous branches shaded the pavement, breaking the monotony of parking lot after parking lot after parking lot. There was a park with a massive old cannon mounted on a cement block facing the bay with a metal plaque on the front. I passed the obligatory Walmart and Home Depot.

The first stoplight I saw turned red. I smiled. The Piggly Wiggly parking lot was right there, and just beyond that I saw the sign for Rocky's Auto Repair. It was a typical garage with four bays, all with their doors open. There was an office to one side with a glass door. A battered looking pickup truck was hoisted up in the air in the first bay. I could see someone underneath working on something about halfway back. The light changed back to green. I waited for an opening in traffic. I turned into the parking lot and stopped my truck right outside the second bay.

I got out of my truck as a guy about my age wearing a filthy pair of torn and baggy jeans came walking out of the building. He was wiping his hands on an oil-covered brick-red rag. A battered and filthy gray tank top with the words *Latona Vikings* on the front barely covered his muscled torso. Wiry black hairs stuck out at the neck. The grimy tank top rode up a bit from his greasy low-hanging jeans, revealing a tan, flat stomach. There was a tattoo of a block-figured cross on his right bicep. It jumped as the muscle flexed and relaxed and flexed again as he kept wiping his hands on the rag. A grimy baseball cap turned backward perched on top of his head. Thick, wavy black hair with hints of dark blue dropped from underneath it almost to his shoulders. There was a smudge of black oil on his cheek just beneath his sharp cheekbones. The shape of his head, the color of his hair, and the deep red tint under his tan spoke of Native American heritage somewhere in his past. Both cheeks and his chin were covered with bluish-black stubble giving his skin a bruised look. His jaw was square with a dimple in the center of his chin. He had a strong nose. Wide set bright blue eyes slanted slightly up at the corners. His chest and shoulders were thick and strong. Bluish thick veins ran across his big biceps and powerful forearms.

I stiffened as he smirked at me. I knew guys like him back home. They were the ones who were too cool for sports, hung out back behind the shop smoking cigarettes at lunch, and bullied kids they decided were weird.

"What's the problem?" he drawled, shoving the rag into his right pants pocket. "That's a pretty old truck, bud."

"Almost two hundred thousand miles." I explained the weird coughing noise I'd heard. "And it doesn't accelerate the way it should, like first gear is slipping or something." I said a silent prayer that the transmission wasn't starting to go. I'd be screwed if that happened.

"Keys." He stuck out his big right hand. There was another tattoo on the inside of his wrist. It looked like a muscular man with a scaly green fish tail.

A merman.

I handed him the keys. "You think you can get to it today?"

He smirked again. "Not like we're swamped with work." He gestured over his shoulder with his thumb. "I'll check it out and give you a call." He pulled a smartphone out of his pants pocket. He touched the screen and asked me for my name and address.

I gave him my name. "I'm staying at Mermaid Inn. Do you want my home address?"

He looked at me for a moment before finishing typing on his screen. "You the new lifeguard?"

I nodded.

"Got a cell number?" he asked. He typed it in as I recited the numbers from memory.

"You'll call me before you do any work?" I asked. "I can only afford so much."

"Sounds to me like you might just have some spark plug problems." He shrugged, the muscular shoulders moving up and down. "I'll take a look and give you a call. Shouldn't take me long. It may need a tune-up. But if it's just the spark plugs that won't cost you too much."

I nodded. "I'll just go get something to eat while I wait. Can you recommend a place? I don't want any fast food."

He gave me an appraising look. "You a swimmer?"

"What gave me away?"

"You're built like one." He smiled. He was actually pretty handsome. The planes of his face relaxed. The dimple in his chin deepened and two more appeared in his cheeks. The blue eyes flashed. His teeth were white and even. "Long arms, flat but strong torso."

"I'm going to Alabama this fall. Scholarship."

"You need a gym?" One of the thick black eyebrows went up. "Bayside Fitness is the best gym in town." He laughed. "Only gym in town besides the Y, and the Y hasn't got new equipment since World War II. Micah, the owner, he'll cut you a deal for a summer membership. Pretty nice guy. Used to be a pro wrestler."

"That's interesting."

"Yeah, they say he could have been a big star if he hadn't gotten injured." He gestured with his head. "You turn into town at that light and drive a couple of blocks. You can't miss it."

"I'll check it out. You were going to recommend a place for me to get some lunch?"

"There's a diner about half a block from here." He shrugged his shoulders slightly. "It's pretty good. Mostly seafood, all fresh caught, and you can get stuff there not fried. But the fried stuff is pretty good. You okay with that?"

"I don't mind fried. I just don't like chains."

He pointed up the road in the opposite direction of Mermaid Inn. "Just head down the sidewalk. You can't miss it. It's called the Singing Mermaid."

*This place sure plays up the mermaid shit,* I thought. *Does everyone here have a mermaid-type tattoo? And where are all the people? This place should be crawling with tourists.*

One summer when I was fourteen Dad had taken me to Destin on the Florida Panhandle for a few days. The traffic had been stop-and-go, the sidewalks crowded—you couldn't turn around without bumping into someone. The beach had been wall-to-wall people with barely any open patches of sand to walk on to get to the water.

*What is wrong with this place?*

"Thanks," I said aloud. I started walking down the sidewalk in the direction he'd indicated. He started up my truck. I looked back over my shoulder as he drove it into the second bay.

It didn't feel quite as hot in town. There was a nice salty breeze blowing off the bay. It felt good to be walking. My legs still felt cramped and tight from the drive. It felt good to stretch them. I walked past a dry cleaner's and a convenience store. People politely waved to me. It seemed like a friendly enough little town. I was starting to get a bit thirsty when I saw the sign for the Singing Mermaid. It wasn't much farther of a walk so I figured I could make it that far.

I had to cross the entry to the parking lot for a massive Lowe's to get to the Singing Mermaid's parking lot.

The Singing Mermaid sat behind an unpaved shell-strewn parking lot. The shells crunched beneath my feet as I walked across them. It was a low wooden building with a rusted tin roof and big, dark plate-glass windows crowded with neon beer signs. Michelob and Coors and Budweiser and Sam Adams flashed their colors onto the crushed gray shells. The lot was empty other than a couple of cars. They sported Alabama plates and had seen better days. One's rear window was cobwebbed with cracks, and the other car had holes rusted into its fenders. Both were coated with dried red dirt all over the doors and the sides. An enormous live oak cast shade in a far corner of the lot. A huge old green Ford pickup truck pulled into the lot as I walked toward the door. It stopped, and a man with scrawny legs beneath a balloon-like torso slid out of the driver's side. He was wearing a flannel shirt and faded jeans. A woman in a tight black skirt with enormous bleached-blond hair got out of the other door with a cigarette dangling from her lips. She smiled at me, her lips a smear of bright red lipstick. They went through the front door. While it was open I could hear an old Reba McEntire song blaring inside.

The air was heavy with grease overpowering the smell of the bay water. I pushed open the door and cold air washed over me. Reba was still singing about her one fine red dress. There was a podium just inside the door with a sign on it reading *seat yourself.* As my eyes adjusted to the dim light I could see there was a bar to my right with liquor bottles lined up behind it. Several glass-fronted coolers filled with beer lined the cheap paneled walls. There was also a swinging door. An older overweight balding man was wiping down the bar. Tables lined the wall along the windows and the far wall. A single row of round tables went down the direct center. An old-style jukebox with bubble tubes stood in a back corner. As I moved toward one of the scarred wooden tables along the windows, Reba stopped singing. After a moment of silence Brad Paisley started singing about some crazy woman who thought his tractor was sexy. The couple who'd just come in sat on the other side of the room. I sat at the second table alongside the windows facing the door.

My stomach rumbled from the smell of frying food. A girl wearing a pair of khaki shorts, white Keds, and a black T-shirt with *The Singing Mermaid* written across her chest in glittery script slapped a red plastic cup of ice water in front of me. Her nametag read Alana. She was olive skinned with almond-shaped green eyes set far apart in her heart-shaped face. Her thick black hair was pulled back into a ponytail that almost reached her waist. She was slender but strong looking. Her tanned legs were muscular. Her breasts were small but firm, her waist narrow. A red apron with pockets was tied low around her waist. She was about five five. There was a bounce to her step that screamed *cheerleader.* She flashed a crooked grin at me as she handed me a laminated menu. "Something to drink?" Her voice was low and soft with a touch of an accent.

She might be working as a waitress, but I'd bet good money she'd been homecoming queen and every boy at Latona High had wanted her.

"Can I get some sweet tea with lemon?" I said after downing the glass of water. I smiled back at her and put the red plastic cup back down. "Lots of lemon."

"Sure can. Our special today is the Mermaid platter," she said briskly, and then laughed. "It's our special every day, actually, but it's a really good deal, especially if you're hungry. Hush puppies, fries, coleslaw, some shrimp, two pieces of catfish, and a couple of butter rolls, for $6.99."

"That sounds perfect," I said, passing the menu back to her without looking at it. She pulled a notepad out of the apron around her waist and made a quick note.

"All right then, I'll be back with your tea in a sec," she said with a wink. I watched her move efficiently across the cement floor to the swinging door by the bar. *Definitely a cheerleader,* I thought. *You only get that kind of bounce in your step from being one.*

I could totally see her on the sidelines of a football game in a pleated skirt and a sweater. The ponytail would be tied with a ribbon in school colors. All the guys in the stands would have their eyes on her the whole game, but her heart would belong to the captain of the football team. They'd make a beautiful couple. He'd be tall and muscular and handsome, maybe with dimples in his cheeks. They'd be the Golden Couple, homecoming king and queen, popular and liked by everyone, nice even to kids like me.

All the girls would be jealous of her, but she was too nice and friendly for them to hate her. They all wanted to be her.

Even if it meant waiting tables in a greasy seafood place every summer.

I looked out the darkened window to the docks on the other side of the road. The sky was completely clear. No feathery wisps of white cloud drifting in the vast expanse of blue. The bay itself looked calm. The waves rolled in without cresting. In the distance there was an occasional flash of white foam, gone almost as suddenly as it appeared. Car after car meandered past on Shore Road, both directions with no sense of hurry. People just seemed to be going about their normal Thursday afternoons. Grocery shopping or running errands, picking up their dry cleaning or gassing up their cars or stopping in for something to eat. Normal everyday people living their daily lives like everyone else in every other little town in every other county.

And Latona seemed like a nice little town. Not much different from Corinth, really. Quiet and laid back, it seemed the perfect place for me to spend the summer before moving into the dorms in Tuscaloosa in August. Brad Paisley finished singing and was replaced by an old song by the Judds. The door opened and a sunburned old man in filthy coveralls walked in. He sat down at the bar. The bartender opened a sweating bottle of beer and set it on a paper napkin in front of him. Neither said a word. The door to the kitchen swung open again and the waitress—Alana—came through. She was carrying a big clear plastic glass and a paper-wrapped straw in one hand. She smiled when she caught me watching her. The red apron bounced as she walked on the balls of her feet. She placed the glass in front of me and handed me the wrapper. "So, you just passin' through?" she asked, resting all of her weight on her right leg and thrusting her hip out a bit.

"Nope. Working here for the summer."

A shadow crossed her face so fast I might have just imagined it. "Where?"

"Lifeguarding at Mermaid Inn." I stuck the straw into the glass and took a drink. It was good tea, with the right amount of sugar. It wasn't overly sweet the way the diner back home in Corinth served. Dad always joked their sweet tea could put you in a diabetic coma.

She nodded, closing her eyes. "Might have known you were a swimmer, with those wide shoulders and long arms." She laughed lightly. She was flirting in a polite way. Just enough to get a better tip but not enough to give me the wrong idea.

Yes, she was definitely head cheerleader material.

"I'm kind of surprised there's no one down at the beach at this time of year." I fiddled with the straw a bit. "Does Latona not get a lot of tourists? I figured with all that beach..."

"Most people head over to Gulf Shores." She shrugged. "Latona's kind of a one-horse town, you know. The only people who come here are the ones who waited too long to make their plans and everywhere else is booked up already or too expensive. We get the cheap tourists here." She made a face. "We're not technically the Gulf here—Mermaid Bay's just an inlet off Mobile Bay." She rolled her eyes. "People want to be on the actual Gulf, I guess."

"Oh." I toyed with the straw a bit more. "Why's it called Mermaid Bay?"

She laughed. "The Native Americans around here thought mermaids lived out in these waters." Again she made the little shrugging motion. "They avoided the place, they thought the mermaids were dangerous. Superstitious. So when the Spanish came here they called it that when they settled the town. There's a legend the mermaids protect us from bad storms. Stupid stuff—they demand human sacrifice in exchange." She wiped her hands on her apron. "Let me go check on your order." She spun on her toes and beat a hasty retreat back through the saloon doors.

I took another drink out of my tea. *Mermaids? Human sacrifice?*

What was it Cecily had said? *We don't have much luck with lifeguards.*

I laughed at myself. *Yeah, Ricky, that's it. There's mermaids out in the bay thirsting for human blood, waiting for lifeguards.*

Like that story about the town we had to read, where they picked someone every year to stone to death.

Ridiculous.

When Alana came back a few minutes later, she was carrying a big plastic plate piled high with steaming-hot fried food. She put it down in front of me and pulled out a couple of bottles from her apron pockets. One was tartar sauce, the other was ketchup. She slapped them down on the table. "You want extra lemons?"

"I'm good." I poured out a puddle of ketchup onto the plate next to the fries.

She started to walk away, and hesitated. "Look—"

"Yeah?"

"Be careful this summer." She looked nervous, eyes darting around to see if anyone in the empty place could hear her.

"What do you mean?"

She shook her head. "Nothing, really. Just—it's just that last summer's lifeguard at Mermaid Inn? He disappeared."

"Disappeared?"

She nodded. "Just vanished one day into thin air." She snapped her fingers. "Like he never existed. Left his clothes and his car behind. Never turned up, either. No one knows what happened to him." She hesitated again. "I'd just hate for something to happen to you, is all. You seem like a nice guy." She spun on her toes again—cheerleading move!—and disappeared back into the kitchen.

*Okay, that's just weird,* I thought, hearing Cecily's voice in my head saying the same thing again. The food smelled amazing, hot and greasy and the batter golden brown. I started eating. I moaned as my mouth watered. The food was good. Lightly battered, fried light and crispy. Hot grease oozed out of the catfish when I used my fork to cut it into pieces. Steam rose. My stomach was insistent, but I refused to give in and start shoveling into my mouth. The grease could burn my tongue and blister the roof of my mouth. I tore open a hot roll and spread butter on it. Finally it was cool enough for me to taste something besides hot. I started shoveling the food in, moaning inwardly with every delicious bite. Usually I tried to eat healthy. Food was fuel for my body, for my muscles, for my workouts. If I ate like this all the time my times would slow down.

But that didn't mean I couldn't enjoy every bite when I allowed myself to break my diet.

When all that was left on my plate was debris, I pushed the plate away and smothered a burp. Alana came over with a plastic pitcher and refilled my tea. "Anything for dessert?"

"No, thanks." I smiled at her. "I'm pretty full. That was really good."

She slapped the bill down on the table. "Pay at the bar."

"Did you know him?"

She looked startled as she slid her pad back into her apron. "Who?"

"The lifeguard. The one who went missing."

She bit her lower lip and nodded. "Yeah. He came in here about once a week before—before, you know. He—he seemed cool." She forced a smile on her face. "Be sure to stop in again sometime." She fled back into the kitchen without another word.

I picked up the bill. I slid a five under my plate for the tip and walked up to the bar after finishing the dregs of the sweet tea. The man with the gray hair rang up my bill and gave me my change without saying anything. I put my wallet back into my shorts pocket and walked back out into the heat. The breeze off the bay had picked up while I was inside. I walked along the sidewalk back to the garage. My truck was parked outside at one of the marked spots. The same guy was working on the same vehicle as before. I went inside the office. The dark-haired guy who I'd talked to was sitting behind the counter, watching a baseball game on a television mounted on the wall.

He nodded at me. "I was right, you just needed new plugs." He slid off the stool and retrieved a clipboard from under the counter. "I also reset the timing for you. Shouldn't have any more trouble. If you do, bring it back in and I'll take care of it. Just ask for Dane."

"Thanks, man." I gave him my debit card, and he ran it. I signed the slip and he handed me the keys.

"You working here this summer?" He asked as he handed me a copy of the work order.

"Lifeguarding at Mermaid Inn. Just got to town today."

He smiled. "Cool. You ever get bored, give me a shout." He shook his head. "This town's pretty fucking dull, man—not much to do except hang out at the Singing Mermaid and a couple of other places. Sometimes me and my buddies head up to Mobile." He stuck out his greasy hand, and I shook it. "Name's Dane Whitsitt."

"Ricky Hackworth."

"Nice to meet you."

He picked up a business card from the tray next to the cash register and handed it to me. "My cell number's on there. Give me a call. I'm always looking for something to do, man."

I put it in my wallet and folded my receipts. "Thanks, man, I'll keep that in mind." At the door I stopped and looked back. "You know a girl who works at the Singing Mermaid named Alana?"

"Everybody knows everybody in Latona, Ricky. Small town, dude." His face split in a grin. "Alana Pavone. She was a couple years behind me at Latona High. She's pretty, and she's single, if that's what you're asking."

"Good to know." I kept my voice casual. "She said something to me about the lifeguard from last summer disappearing?"

His smile vanished. "Yeah. That was kinda weird. Nice guy too." He sat back down on his stool. "He used to go swimming every morning and late at night. He had a scholarship to swim for Bama." He made a little noise. "Everyone pretty much figured he got a cramp or something and drowned. Why else would he leave everything behind the way he did?"

"He never washed up on shore?"

"Undertow might have pulled him out to the main bay. Sharks might have got him." His eyes were veiled. "All kinds of things can happen to someone out in the water, you know."

"Were you guys friends?"

Dane shrugged. "We hung out a couple of times." He gave me a funny look. "You never heard about him disappearing? You got a job down here and you didn't look up anything online?"

"I just found out I got the job yesterday—the guy they originally hired changed his mind." I replied, a bit defensively. "I barely had time to pack. Besides, I was so glad for the chance to get away from Corinth for the summer I didn't want to look a gift horse in the mouth, you know?"

"Corinth?" His eyebrows came together. "Where's that?"

"Middle of nowhere, forty miles off the highway." I laughed. "We don't even have an exit off Highway 59, you know? We'd need a horse to be a one-horse town."

He laughed, flashing strong white teeth at me. "You a swimmer too?"

I nodded. "Yup. Got a scholarship to Bama too. Start this fall."

"Then you need to be careful when you go out swimming. Make sure someone knows you're out there." He shook his head. "People always think the bay's safe because it's a bay. It's still connected to the Gulf. All kinds of predators out there in the water. All kinds."

We just stared at each other for another minute or two, then he broke the mood by grinning at me. "Give me a call if you wanna hang out sometime, Ricky."

I nodded and went out the door.

*Predators. Like mermen? Or people with merman tattoos?*

My truck started right up, and soon cold air was blowing out through the vents. I stopped in at the Piggly Wiggly and got some things I'd need and headed back out to the Inn. The same Subaru was in the parking lot that had been there before, but there was also a new car I didn't recognize, a big black Chevy Tahoe that looked relatively new. I carried my bags up the driveway and headed inside. I lugged them up all the stairs to the top floor and was putting the key into my lock when a man's voice said, "You must be Ricky."

I looked over my shoulder as I unlocked the door and swung it open. "Hey," I said, "come on in." I carried the bags into the kitchenette and set them down on the counter, wiped my hands on my shorts, and stuck out my right hand as he stepped into my room. "You must be Joe Hampton."

"Yeah." He shook my hand vigorously. He was an inch or two shorter than I was, but powerfully built. He was wearing a ripped-up old pair of jeans and an Alabama Crimson Tide gray tank top. He was maybe in his mid to late forties. He was balding, with thin light brown hair on the sides. He was deeply tanned, and there were creases in his face from years of sun and wind exposure. "Welcome to Mermaid Inn. Cecily said she'd kind of given you a bit of a rundown on how things work around here." He laughed. "I bet she didn't tell you about the dumbwaiter, though."

"Dumbwaiter?"

He gestured for me to follow him back out into the hallway. He stopped about halfway down the hall and stepped over to the wall. There was a small handle I hadn't noticed close to the floor. He bent over, grabbed it, and pulled it up. Behind it I could see a flat platform. He grinned at me. "Yeah. No sense in carrying things up the stairs. You just put stuff in here and send it up." He pulled it closed again. "Downstairs just outside the laundry room is where this comes out. There's a button to send it down or send it up. Makes things easier with the laundry and the linens and stuff."

"Good to know."

He straightened back up. "Hope you'll join Cecily and me for dinner tonight. I'm making my specialty, pot roast. Kind of a welcome-to-the-family dinner." He smiled at me.

"Sounds nice."

"Just come on down and knock on our door around seven."

"Great." We walked back down the hall to my door. "I'll do that, Mr. Hampton."

"Just call me Joe." He smiled again. "Glad you're here, Ricky. Hope you enjoy the summer here."

"I'm sure I will." I stepped back into my room. "Well, I should get those groceries put away, and I want to go for a swim. I'll see you at seven tonight, then." *If I don't disappear in the meantime.*

"Okay." He started to turn away, but stopped. "Just be careful."

I closed the door and hesitated for just a moment before locking it.

I exhaled and started putting my groceries away. It didn't take long—I hadn't gotten a lot, figuring I could make another trip in to the Piggly Wiggly if I needed to. I did really want to go for a swim—my muscles felt tight from sitting in the car all morning, and I hated being out of the water for even a day. The groceries stored, I opened my duffel bag and unpacked it, laying my clothes out on the bed before putting them away. I did that quickly, and then changed out of the clothes I was wearing and stuffed them into the duffel bag, which I figured I could use as a laundry basket. I slipped on a racing suit, pulled on a pair of shorts, and found my flip-flops and my swimming goggles. I looked out the window and could see a sailboat pretty far out on the water. I turned and started for the door but dropped my goggles, which bounced across the floor and disappeared under the bed.

I swore and dropped to my stomach. I could see the goggles in the dust under the bed, resting next to a matchbook. I grabbed both and examined the matchbook.

The matchbook was black, and there was a logo of a flexing bicep on the cover.

DUSTY'S, MOBILE. 555-1978.

I opened the cover, and a name was written in a bold scrawl on the inside: *Dane, 555-8007.*

I retrieved the card from my wallet.

It was Dane's cell-phone number.

## CHAPTER THREE

My muscles were tired when I knocked on the Hamptons' door.

I stifled a yawn. My stomach was growling. I'd burned off lunch by going for a long swim and taken a nap.

The tiredness felt great. I liked the feeling of knowing I'd worked hard. I loved pushing my body as hard as I could. And I loved the water. I loved being in the water. I missed it the last couple of days when I hadn't been able to do my twice-a-day workout. In Corinth I swam in the school pool. Every morning for as long as I could remember, I'd gotten out of bed at four. Every morning the same routine of a cup of black coffee, a bowl of brown-sugared oatmeal, a splash of cold water into my face to help clear my head. The drive through the inky blackness of the early morning hour, stars winking overhead in a deep purple sky, to the school. Fumbling for the keys to let myself in. Stripping off my sweats, kicking them aside, letting them collapse to a pile of warm cotton. Shaking out my arms to get the blood flowing, twisting and turning and kicking out my legs front and side. Jumping into the cold chlorinated water, the shock of the welcoming water against my warm skin. Fixing the goggles over my eyes. Warming up slowly by swimming a couple of slow laps. I always can smell the chlorine, in or out of the pool. I always smelled of chlorine, like it had soaked into my skin, like my sweat on hot days was laced with it. It was always in my hair and on my clothes. Chlorine was the smell of my childhood, my growing up. Chlorine defined me.

The water was my home, welcoming me back every time I dove into it.

Chlorinated water didn't judge me for my worn-out cheap clothes, for having a father who couldn't buy me a new car or belong to the country club. Chlorinated water didn't call me names, names whispered or sneered at me as I passed. Whispers and sneers I'd learned early to ignore, to pretend not to hear the giggles and mean-spirited laughter. All that mattered in the water was the stroke, how fast I was going, my endurance, how long I could maintain that speed, and whether I could find another gear when I needed to, when my muscles were filled with burning lactic acid and my lungs gasping, unable to take in enough oxygen, it seemed, to keep me going—unless I focused, unless I forced the air in, as I used my will and determination to push the muscles further and further until my fingertips brushed the wall and the stopwatch was clicked off.

I always preferred the water to land.

And after the slow and steady warm-up laps, getting used to the water again and establishing my breathing rhythm, it was time to work.

Speeding up, swimming faster as I went from one side of the pool to the other, eyes peering through my goggles through the water, counting strokes. One stroke then another and still another. Turning my head to breathe as I did my freestyle laps. The sound of the slap of my feet against the wall echoing through the water as I flipped and turned to go back the other way. Rolling my body from head to toe, clamping my feet together as I shimmered through the water, stretching and kicking and trying to get as far as I could before rising back to the surface and starting the stroke again, counting, always counting. One stroke, two stroke, three stroke, and breathe. Letting muscle memory take over as I went through the water, stroke after stroke, lap after lap. The freestyle stroke, the backstroke, the breaststroke, and the butterfly, so many laps in each stroke, sprints and then slower, trying to make sure the form and technique were perfect.

And finally the cool down, barely moving through the water as my breathing got easier and slower, the heart rate coming down, the adrenaline slowing until I finally climbed out of the water, shivering in the cold as I toweled myself dry and pulled the sweats back on to head home for a massive breakfast to get me through the day before I went back into the water at four.

Swimming in the bay was different than the pool. It had been a couple of days since I'd been able to work out, to push myself the way I wanted to work with all the preparations for the trip down and the summer, saying my good-byes to the few friends I had. The bay water was warm and salty and buoyant. The sand at the bottom gave a bit as I walked out into the water in my Speedo, the goggles in place already over my eyes making everything a bit amber. The sun was getting lower in the western sky, closer to the tops of the pine trees so far in the distance on the other side. Twisting and turning and bouncing on the balls of my feet before taking a deep breath and diving into the waves. The tide was coming in, so I had to fight against it on my way out. When I flipped out there I could relax a bit and let it carry me back to the shallow water, riding with the current instead of against it. It's easy to train in a pool, lap after lap after lap, flip turns with feet slapping against the wall propelling me back against the backwash in the other direction.

But swimming in the bay, the tide and the waves made it harder to make my strokes smooth and easy and rhythmic. I always counted strokes, using the stroke count to determine how tired I was. Less strokes were better, stretching my body out almost to its entire length, reaching and pushing my arms out as far as I could, my back muscles straining as I pulled my body forward. I decided to turn every fifty strokes, because that was a pool length. The last thing I wanted to do was go into the zone and not count, wind up too far out and too tired to swim back. I swam until every muscle was aflame with lactic acid buildup, until my lungs were aching and gasping and my feet felt like lead weights as I finally put them down onto the sandy bottom and stood, climbing out of the water and wrapping the towel around my waist.

I had stood there on the shore, shaking the water out of my hair, slipping my feet into the flip-flops. I'd looked up at the house and seen a movement in one of the windows so slight I might have imagined it. I kept looking, but nothing else happened.

Now, I knocked lightly on the door with my knuckles. I could smell food and my stomach rumbled menacingly. I'd had a protein shake before taking my nap but it wasn't enough to make up for the calories I'd burned in the water.

Cecily opened the door with a disinterested, almost bored look on her face. "Well, come in then," she said impatiently, turning and walking back inside.

I stepped over the threshold and took in their apartment. It was far bigger than mine, running the entire length of the house, longer than it was wide. The floor was polished hardwood, the decor what I thought of as beach style. Polished shells atop surfaces, driftwood sculpture here and there, a fishing net spread over part of the sloping ceiling, with starfish and other shells attached to it. A ship's lantern stood in a corner. Hurricane lamps with blackened wicks sat atop tables and the mantel of the fireplace. The furniture wasn't expensive but was sturdy and good, maybe a generation or so out of style. I could smell garlic and sausage, bread and melted butter. There was a dining table set up lengthwise in front of an enormous eight-foot window, the curtains pulled back and the shutters opened. We were up so high you couldn't see the parking lot or long drive unless you were standing directly in front of the window. The view was of the towering pines and Spanish-moss-adorned live oaks on the other side of the state highway. The sun was low in the sky on the other side of the house, and the sky above the forest was turning an exceptionally beautiful purplish blue with streaks of lighter blue illuminated. It was beautiful, like a painting whose artist had spent hours carefully placing each brushstroke.

Cecily disappeared through a door to one side. When she went through the door the smells became even stronger and my stomach rumbled again. The ache in my empty stomach was so strong I felt almost dizzy for a moment. I stood there, in the living room, not sure what to do or if I should sit down. Another hunger pang made me almost nauseous. The table was set with three places. A basket of buttered and toasted rolls was already placed in the center. I knew it was rude but I helped myself to one, gobbling it down quickly before Cecily or Joe could come back and catch me. It was delicious, homemade with melted garlic butter soaked into it while it cooked.

I fought the urge to have another. My stomach growled again.

"I didn't think to ask you if you liked pasta," Joe said as he came through the door Cecily had disappeared through. He was carrying an enormous colander full of steaming spaghetti noodles. Cecily followed him with another bowl, full of red sauce with chunks of onions and bell peppers and fried sausage floating in its thickness. "But I figured everyone loves pasta. You don't have any allergies?"

"No, sir," I replied. "And that sure smells good." My stomach rumbled loud enough for him to hear, and he grinned back at me.

"Someone forgot to thaw out the pot roast," Cecily said as she placed the bowl of sauce down next to the basket of rolls. She rolled her eyes.

"Just means you'll have to come back over when I make my famous pot roast." Joe smiled as he put the pasta down and pulled out the chair with its back to the window. "Have a seat." He gestured to the chair once everything was set out on the table.

I sat and helped myself to a big plate full of spaghetti. I ladled sauce onto it and mixed it in with my fork. I sprinkled parmesan cheese over the top, and grabbed a couple of the rolls. Cecily passed me a sweating pitcher of iced tea, and I filled my glass. I waited until they had both served themselves before dipping a roll into the sauce. It was delicious—spicy and hot and full of flavor. "Wow," I said after I swallowed, "this sauce is amazing."

"I'm not much of a cook," Joe admitted as he twisted several strands of spaghetti around his fork, "but the things I can make, I am really good at. Sauce is one of those things."

"I'm the cook around here," Cecily said, not smiling or putting any inflection in her tone. "But he let me have the night off." She never looked up from her plate.

I didn't know what to say to that, so I focused on curling spaghetti onto my fork.

"I saw you went for a swim," Joe said into the silence that followed. "Is it a lot different out in the water than in a pool? You have a scholarship, right?"

"Yes, sir," I said, dipping another roll in the sauce. It was so incredibly delicious I wanted to just keep dipping rolls into it until there weren't any left. "I have a scholarship to Alabama." I shrugged. "It's not going to pay for everything, so I need to make as much as I can during the summer break. I was going to work for my dad this summer, but I'm glad this opportunity came up. Dad does his best, but he can't pay me very much." I grabbed another roll. "And there's differences, sure, between the bay and a pool. But swimming is swimming, you know? And as long as I can practice my strokes and keep my endurance up, I'm good. I do need to find a gym so I can get back on the weights too."

"The only real pool in Latona is at the country club." Joe's tone was apologetic. "I can see if they'd let you swim laps there—"

"No need, sir." I started twisting some spaghetti onto my fork, and then speared a mushroom with the prongs. "The bay works just fine."

"Bayside Fitness and the Y are the only gyms in Latona." Cecily sprinkled more parmesan cheese on her spaghetti. "The Y's a dump, though. Or you can drive up to Mobile. Lots of choices there."

"I'm going to check out Bayside," I said, helping myself to more spaghetti and sauce.

The conversation died down. The only sounds were fork tines scraping against plates, tea being drunk, and pasta being chewed. I mopped up sauce with another roll when I finished my second helping of pasta, then added just a bit more to my plate.

"Have more," Joe said when I put the bowl down. "I'm pretty full, and Cecily never has seconds, and I'll just wind up throwing it out. I can save the sauce but pasta doesn't really last, you know?"

"You sure?" I refilled my plate.

"You must have to eat a lot," Joe observed. "With all the swimming—how much do you usually do?"

"I try to swim every morning and every evening. I also try to do strength conditioning with weights at least three times a week. I do burn a lot of calories."

Cecily took her plate into the kitchen without saying anything. After the door shut I could hear running water.

"She doesn't seem to like me much," I said, taking another roll. "Did I do something?"

Joe sighed and ran his hands through his hair. "Don't mind her, Ricky. It takes her a while to warm up to people. Ever since her parents—" He broke off when the kitchen door swung open again, and his face reddened.

"Go ahead, Uncle Joe." Cecily's voice was flat, her face expressionless. She slipped back into her chair and put her elbows up on the table, supporting her chin on her fists. "You can tell him, he's going to find out soon enough."

He didn't say anything. Instead he picked up his tea and took another drink. He kept his eyes on the table.

She turned to me. "Ever since my parents were killed, is what he was going to say, since you want to know. My parents and my brother, if you need to know the body count. My whole family. I wasn't with them. I was sick and home with a babysitter. They went to a movie without me. A drunk driver killed them on their way home. They stopped to get me ice cream as a treat for having to skip the movie. They called me right before they left the theater to see what I wanted." Her eyes remained flat, her tone cold. It was like she was standing in front of a classroom reciting a lesson in an emotionless monotone. "So I sat there on the couch under a blanket waiting for them to come home with my cookies-and-cream ice cream. Instead, the highway patrol showed up and told me I was an orphan. Luckiest flu I've ever had." Her eyes were glassy. "And I came to live here with my only living relative. We're all we've got, right, Uncle Joe?"

He reached over to take her hand, but she pulled away from his reach. And looked away from him.

"My mother died when I was seven," I replied, looking squarely into her hazel eyes. "Cancer. She was sick almost from the time I was born. I don't remember her much except for being sick and in the hospital. It was just me and my dad pretty much my whole life."

Her face softened, but only a little bit. "So you know." It was barely above a whisper.

*You lost yours suddenly. I had to watch my mother die when I was a little boy.*

I closed my eyes and I was back there in the hospital. The smell of bleach and antiseptic, the beeping of the machines, the smell…

I opened my eyes. "I started swimming right after she died. I like it. I like being out there in the water by myself. It's just me, me and the water, and it's all on me, how hard I swim and how fast. I don't like swimming relays. I only do it when Coach makes me."

She looked at me intently but didn't say anything. She pushed her chair back and stood. She reached over and grabbed my plate. I could smell her perfume—she smelled vaguely of lilies of the valley. She stacked her uncle's plate on top of mine. "We've got chocolate cake for dessert, if you want some."

I was full, uncomfortably so. I took a deep breath and was going to say no. But when I opened my mouth to say so, I noticed Joe giving me a look and a slight nod of his head. "Yeah, that would be great." I smiled at her. "Could I get a glass of milk to go with it? If it's not too much trouble?"

She nodded and picked up the almost empty tea pitcher. Once the kitchen door swung shut behind her again, he whispered across the table, "It's only been a couple of years, Ricky. So don't be too hard on her. She's still healing. She's a little prickly, but she's a very sweet girl once you get to know her."

I nodded. *How do you get to know someone who's so unfriendly? If she would even give me a chance…I'm not going to go out of my way with her.*

But instead I plastered my friendliest and biggest smile on my face when she came back carrying two small plates with healthy slices of red velvet cake on them, and a tall glass of milk. She set a plate down in front of Joe and put the other plate and glass of milk in front of me. "Aren't you having any?" I frowned.

"I'm full." She shook her head. It was delicious, probably the best cake I've ever had. We ate our dessert again in silence, and when it was finished, I pushed my chair back and stood.

"Thank you for dinner," I said. "I'll get out of your way now. Unless—do you want me to do the dishes? I'd be happy to, it's the least I can do as payment for such a good meal."

"Don't be ridiculous, you're a guest," Joe replied. "And you're welcome to stay as long as you like."

"I'm kind of beat," I said, putting my hand over my mouth as I yawned. "Long day, and I want to get up early and go for a swim."

Joe got up and shook my hand, but Cecily didn't say anything, just cleared the table and headed into the kitchen, the door shutting behind her with a determined bang.

"If you need anything, just let us know," Joe said to me at the door. "I hope you enjoy your summer here with us. If there's anything we can do to make you feel more at home, you let us know, okay?"

"Thanks. I'll do that." I noticed he didn't shut his door until I was inside my room and closing mine.

*Weird.*

I wiped sweat off my forehead. The sun had gone down, and it was just past nine. I yawned again. I got a bottle of water out of the refrigerator and stretched. *It was going to feel good to go to sleep,* I thought, remembering to set the alarm on my phone to wake me at five.

I sat down at the little desk and opened my laptop. I scrolled through Facebook before checking my e-mails. In my Gmail inbox there was one from my father:

*Ricky,*

*I guess I understand what you're doing and why you're doing it, but that doesn't make the house any less lonely without you in it. I suppose it was bound to happen, you couldn't keep living at home for the rest of your life, but that doesn't mean I have to like it any more than I do. I just tell myself to think you're off at swim camp, but I know you're not going to be coming home for good. Just remember to be careful, son, and don't hesitate to call me if you need anything. I'll try not to worry, but it's not easy.*

*I love you,*
*Dad*

Tears came up in my eyes. I wiped them away. I got up and walked away from the laptop. I leaned against the sloping ceiling. It had been just the two of us for so long…I know he'd hoped after I got the scholarship to Bama I might commute—Tuscaloosa was only about a forty-minute drive from Corinth—but with swim practice and everything else it wasn't practical. Not if I wanted to make grades. It would be cheaper, sure. I'd gone over it all in my head I don't know how many times before I made the decision to live on campus. I hated leaving Dad. It just didn't make sense to commute.

I bit my lower lip, and in that moment I was more lonesome than I could remember. It was worse than the first time I'd gone to swim camp. Mom had been gone a few years. Dad was all I had, but the swimming coach thought I needed to go to swim camp. I remember when he talked to me and Dad in his office at the high school.

"Ricky is a natural," Coach Marren had said that afternoon. "I think going to swim camp, getting some instruction from top coaches and being around other kids who are training to be champions, will do him some good. He might be good enough to go all the way, Mr. Hackworth, to the Olympics. I've never seen a kid with so much potential for swimming. I know it's expensive, but it'll pay off in the long run. If he doesn't become an Olympian, he'll get a scholarship for college at the very least…"

Dad asked me if I wanted to go. I said yes.

The water. I was always at home in the water. In the water nobody feels sorry for you because you're a poor little motherless kid. No one makes fun of you because they think you dress funny or your voice is too high-pitched or maybe you aren't as masculine as they think you should be. But that first night, after getting on the bus that took me and my suitcase to Tuscaloosa for a two-week intensive swimming training camp, alone in the little dorm room I was sharing with some rich kid, I cried myself to sleep. I cried because I missed my dad and because my mother was gone. After that I was too tired to be lonesome for home.

I took a deep breath. I sat back down and wrote back that I was fine, missed him, and would let him know if I needed anything.

My dad was the greatest. He'd always made it to every one of my swim meets. He was always there for me.

If he worried about me, he kept it to himself. I know he wondered sometimes about me not having friends, not going to the prom, not going to football games or anything like that. None of that interested me. I wanted to get good grades and I wanted to swim.

That was all that ever mattered to me.

I went back to my Facebook page. Most of my friends there were kids from school or guys I'd met at swim camp or swam against, become friends with from seeing them here and there, this meet or that one. I scrolled through the News Feed. Nothing, more nothing, and still more nothing.

I scratched my chin and impulsively pulled up Google. I typed in *Dusty's Mobile* but nothing came up.

I closed my laptop and walked over to the window. There was some condensation on the pane, and there were some dark clouds over the bay in the distance, coming closer. I opened the window and got a blast of heat and humidity right in the face—but the air felt thick and heavy, like a storm was coming. As I watched, some lightning flashed in the distance. I counted to twenty before I heard the distant thunder. I started to close the window when I heard a sound out on the roof. I leaned out the window and looked in either direction. The roof slanted down from the window at about a forty-five degree angle, from the peak at the top. The sound I'd heard had come from the other side of the roof, which I couldn't see from this window unless I climbed out there, onto the tiles. I heard another sound and pushed the window up all the way. I turned my back to the sill and sat on it, swinging my legs up and around and then out the window. I slid out onto the hot tiles, still sitting on the sill.

There—I heard it again.

It must just be seagulls—there were certainly plenty of them around. But I wasn't afraid of heights and the view was spectacular from the windowsill. The bay itself was getting rougher. Big whitecaps were curling and breaking against the white sand beach. The waves were bigger than the ones when I went for my swim. Some of them looked to be as much as ten feet high, the trough in front of the wave becoming shallower as the wave sucked water up into the curling lip of foam. There was another streak of lightning on the other side of the bay. There were no boats out there. The moon was nearly full but hidden by the fast-moving, dark clouds. Every once in a while the moon would break through a hole in the clouds, bathing the bay with its luminescence. I closed my eyes and allowed the rhythmic, hypnotic sound of the waves to lull me a little bit.

"Hey," Cecily's voice said from behind me, startling me so much that I jumped and almost slid off the ledge. "Sorry—didn't mean to scare you." She came down around the gable of the window and sat next to me on the sill. "Uncle Joe's watching a baseball game, and I got a little bored."

"You climb over the roof a lot?"

"I like it up here, when it's cool in the evenings," she said. "I watch the sun set over the bay a lot. No one uses your room, you know, when we don't have a lifeguard staying here, so I just come over and push the window up and have a seat and watch. It's peaceful."

"Sorry about your family."

"Sorry about your mom."

I shrugged. "I was young. It was over ten years ago."

"You don't miss her?"

"Of course I do. But it stopped hurting a long time ago."

"It's been three years," she replied. "Uncle Joe, the counselor, everyone tells me it'll stop hurting at some point, but I'd like to know when."

"Everyone heals at a different speed. There's no time limit."

"Yeah, well."

"Can I ask you something?"

"Yeah, go ahead."

"When I was in town today, a couple of people mentioned the lifeguard from last summer."

She stiffened a little bit. "Zach Patterson." She exhaled explosively. "He disappeared. I guess I should have told you about him before someone else did. It's kind of an awkward subject."

"He disappeared? What do you mean, he disappeared?"

She nodded. "Yup. He just up and vanished without a trace one night. Left everything behind, even his car." She rolled her eyes. "Cops could never figure it out, you know. FBI agents even came down to look into it. His parents made a stink. Uncle Joe thinks it's why bookings are off this summer."

"Is that why the other lifeguard you guys hired quit at the last minute?"

She shrugged. "Maybe. I don't know. I don't think he gave Uncle Joe a reason. Would you have taken the job had you known?"

I thought for a moment. "Probably. I mean, what are the odds?" As soon as the words left my mouth I felt a chill go down my spine. "But it would have been nice to know before I got here, you know."

She peered at me. "I figured you hadn't heard about it, otherwise you wouldn't have applied for the job." She gave a laugh. "You were one of the only people who applied." She shook her head and sighed. "I don't know what happened to him. I wish I did. He was a nice guy. A bit on the arrogant side, but a nice guy all the same." She looked off into the distance. "Sometimes I used to come over here and we'd sit and watch the sun go down, and talk. He was a nice guy, really." She sighed. "You get your truck all taken care of?"

"Yeah, it just needed spark plugs."

She narrowed her eyes. "Did you meet Dane Whitsitt?"

I nodded. "Yeah. Seemed nice."

"He's not nice." She folded her arms. "Not nice at all."

"Did what's his name—Zach—know him?"

She nodded. "Yeah, Zach knew him. They hung out a bit before he disappeared."

The storm clouds were moving faster now, toward us from across the bay, and it was getting darker. "People don't just disappear."

She gave a hollow laugh and stood back up again. "People disappear all the time, Ricky." It was the first time she'd said my name, and she had a sour look on her face as she dusted off her hands. "I'm getting back inside before that storm gets here. You'd best do the same."

Without another word she started climbing back up the slope of the roof.

I sat there for another few moments, until the clouds were almost to the shore, and then slid back through the window, closing it behind me just as the first drops of rain hit the roof.

I pulled the matchbook out of my pocket and stared at it again.

# Chapter Four

My nightmares are always about water.

I never dream about drowning. Even when asleep, my mind doesn't forget I spend as much time as I can in the water. No, I never dream about drowning. I never worry about tiring or cramping. I never worry about sinking below the surface and my lungs filling with water as my life flashes before my eyes. When I was younger, I used to always see how long I could stay under before my lungs ached and my body screamed for air.

No, I've never been afraid of drowning.

The nightmares are always about *things* in the water. Monsters. Sea creatures. Sharks speeding through the water with their vicious teeth exposed and bloodlust for human flesh. Stingrays with their razor-wire tails that can slash through flesh right to the bone. Giant squid or octopi squirting out black ink to cloud the water so I can't see their waving tentacles coming through the water to wrap around me and squeeze out my breath as they draw me into their beaked mouths. The vicious teeth of a school of barracuda, slashing through the water from out of nowhere and tearing chunks of flesh from my body. Giant crabs and lobsters scuttling along the bottom, waving enormous razor-sharp claws as they come after me. An enormous water moccasin, fangs dripping venom, chasing after me through the orange-stained river at the back boundary of my grandfather's farm and biting me again and again while I writhe and scream. It's always some variation of the same thing. I am always pursued by something vicious and bloodthirsty in the water. Of course, the older I've gotten the less frequently I have bad dreams. Usually they are triggered by a change in my environment. I always seem to have them the first night of swim camp. I don't know if it's because I'm not in my own bed—but it always happens. So my first night at Mermaid Inn, I was sort of expecting to have one when I tumbled exhausted in my bed.

But the one I had that first night was a new one. And it was one of the worst I've ever had.

The thunderstorm had broken in its full fury by the time I'd brushed my teeth and washed my face. I walked out of the bathroom as lightning flashed so close to the building that my entire room lit up with a blinding white light that left spots dancing in front of my eyes. The crack of thunder that followed shook the building, rattling my back teeth. The slight sprinkle became a deluge. I slid into my bed and closed my eyes, listening to the pounding of the water on the roof just above my head.

The next thing I knew, I was out swimming in the bay, skimming across the surface, rising with the peak of the gentle waves and then sinking back into the trough between. I was wearing my goggles and trying to take as many strokes as possible without breathing. It's an exercise, trying to build lung capacity and endurance. You can't do it all the time because you don't want to make it second nature so you wind up not breathing regularly during a meet when your muscles are aching and screaming for oxygen. When you're racing, you want to breathe every other stroke, if not on every stroke. I have great lung capacity. I can swim from one end of the pool to the other completely underwater without straining for air. I can also inhale a lot of oxygen in the few seconds per stroke when my mouth comes up.

The sun was shining high in the sky as I knifed cleanly through the mostly calm water. I kept my eyes focused on the white sand at the bottom. I was doing freestyle. My right arm swung up and back into the water as my left arm came up to repeat the stroke. An occasional large fish would dart by underneath me, scales flashing when hit by the sunlight diffusing through the green water. Crabs scuttled along the bottom. Schools of minnows darted around. An occasional multicolored jellyfish about the size of a quarter would undulate beneath me. Occasionally I would spot a rusted can or a bottle half-buried in the sand. Every so often I'd spy a patch of seaweed waving in the current. I kept swimming farther out from the shore. I kept holding my breath, stroke after stroke. Right then left and right again. I focused on keeping my head down in the water while flipping my wrist down into the water as my forward hand came back into the water on the forward stroke. My muscles were aching as I kicked with my legs and dragged my body through the warm salty water, the sun burning into my back as I twisted from side to side with every stroke and movement of my arms. The bay floor began to drop farther and farther away from the surface as I moved out to the center of the bay, making it more and more difficult to see bottom as the water became darker and deeper.

Out of the corner of my eye, I saw a large shape dart into my sight line. I felt a chill go down my spine as I turned my head to get a better look because the shape was so large. I immediately stopped my forward motion and let my legs drift down beneath me, treading water as I squinted through the gloom to make sure it wasn't a shark, my heart pounding in my ears.

But it wasn't a shark I saw. It had a long tail, yes, but what I was seeing wasn't a shark's tail.

It was a mermaid.

My fear began to fade away and curiosity rose. I kept watching. The tail was quite large, wide and greenish and sideways in the water, unlike a shark's tail.

*Mermaids aren't real, they're mythological creatures,* I reminded myself in the dream.

*The Native Americans used to believe the mermaids demanded human sacrifice.*

The fear came back. Every instinct in my body told me to turn and swim as hard as I could, back for the shore.

But I couldn't move. I continued to hover there in the water, peering through my goggles, watching the creature that couldn't possibly exist, that I couldn't possibly be seeing.

The mermaid turned in the water in a slow graceful movement. To my shock I saw it wasn't actually a maid but rather a man. He was still too far away for me to make out his facial features, but there was definitely a full beard. His long hair drifted around his head in the water as he maneuvered himself into a standing position, his tail occasionally flicking to keep himself erect in the gloomy water beneath me. His long grayish arms began beckoning to me to swim down and join him. His torso was muscular and strong. His shoulders were wide. His pecs were thick and his nipples were enormous. His torso tapered down into an almost ridiculously narrow waist before his skin turned into scales. The scales were an odd combination of blue and green and gray, the colors changing and sparkling in the dim light from the surface. They were hypnotically beautiful as they changed colors with every flick of his tail. It might have been just a trick of the weak light under the surface, but I couldn't seem to look away.

He beckoned again, his arm waving through the water. When I didn't move, he opened his mouth and started singing to me.

I'd never heard anything like his sound before.

If there were words, I couldn't understand them. It was just notes, sound.

It was the most beautiful thing I could ever remember hearing. His voice was magical, pure and crystalline and clear. The beauty of the sound was almost too painful to listen to. The notes he sang went through me like arrows piercing my skin, my soul, my heart. The tone washed over me, into me, and set every nerve tingling. The exquisite tonality brought tears to my eyes, goose bumps up on my skin, and a feeling of ecstasy unlike anything I'd ever experienced before. I couldn't move a muscle. I didn't *want* to move. I just floated there, suspended in the water, my eyes wide open and staring at him as he continued to sing. His face somehow became clear to me through the murkiness of the water. The beard floated out from his face. He had a strong jaw, high cheekbones. His nose was aquiline. His eyes were green, enormous and beautiful. I could get lost in them. I couldn't stop looking at him…

*Come with me and be my love.*

The notes reverberated through the water. He was still beckoning to me with his beautiful hands. The fingers were so graceful and long. I wasn't aware of anything else except him. He wanted me to follow him deeper into the water, farther away from the shore, and intimated that somehow everything would be not only all right but things would be better. No more poverty. No more sadness and pain. Everything would be forgotten if I just swam down and joined him. And I wanted to. I desperately wanted to. I wanted to leave everything behind. I couldn't think of anything else but the voice, the beautiful purity of the voice. He would make everything all right.

I tried.

I tried to kick my legs and arrow down through the water.

Yet somehow I couldn't move anything.

It was like the notes he was singing had paralyzed me.

I closed my eyes.

*How would you breathe? You can't live under the water.*

As haunting and beautiful as the music was, I couldn't join him.

My father's face...

I couldn't leave him behind.

I was all he had.

*If you come with me you won't need air to live. Your father will go on. He could find love again, you know. Has it ever occurred to you that you're the reason he has never remarried?*

Doubt filled me.

I had thought that before, had wondered. Dad was so lonely. He was still young, why didn't he date? Why didn't he find another woman to love? I never wanted to believe it was my fault, that it was because of me he had remained unmarried...

But I was gone for the summer, about to be gone for college.

*Come with me and you will be happy.*

Yet still I didn't move, much as I yearned to.

I opened my eyes.

I continued to float there. He stopped beckoning and started moving toward me, gracefully gliding through the water, the big smile still in place on his face, which was even more handsome than

I'd thought as he came closer. Muscles rippled and flowed beneath the pale skin, which became whiter, like marble, as he moved into water more lit by the sun. I could see blue veins pulsing under the skin in his arms, his chest. There was no hair on his torso, and I felt lust, desire, need course through me in just a matter of moments.

He stopped moving when he was about ten feet below me, the greenish-blue eyes sparkling in the sunlight, his stunning beauty almost blinding me as I stared at him, his mouth still smiling as he continued to sing, the notes louder than before, moving like a current through the warm water. My hair stood up, the follicles tingling—my skin felt warm like I was getting a fever. He reached his hands out to me and beckoned again.

Again I refused.

The smile faded and he stopped singing.

His eyes narrowed and began to glow yellow.

The ecstasy turned to terror in an instant.

Every instinct in my body was screaming at me to turn around and swim as fast as my muscles could move me toward the shore.

Yet I wasn't able to do anything other than stare.

Stare as his lips drew back from his teeth in a snarl.

His sharp, long, pointed teeth.

His hands reached for me.

I hadn't noticed that his fingernails were also long, sharp, and pointed.

His hands grabbed my upper arms—

—and I sat up in my bed, gasping for breath.

It was still raining, drumming a steady tattoo on the roof. It was pitch-black inside my room. The window in the gable looked like a black velvet curtain had been dropped over it. I sat there, trying to calm my breathing and the pounding of my heartbeat. *What the hell?* I thought, glancing over at the digital clock on the bedside table. It was blinking *12:00* at me in red. I swallowed and reached in the darkness for where I'd left my phone. I wrapped my hand around it and picked it up. I touched the screen and the keypad came up, as well as the time: 3:12 a.m.

My heart was still pounding even though I had my breathing now under control. I focused on breathing. In, out, in, out, long and deep and slow. It took a few minutes for my heart rate to slow to a more normal pace. I swung my legs around to put my feet on the floor and stood up in the darkness. The windows were being pelted, the water sluicing down in streams. I turned on the bedside lamp. I went into the kitchenette in my briefs and got a glass of water. My alarm was set for six. I wanted to get back into my habit of swimming early in the morning. But if it was raining...I sighed. *Maybe swimming in the bay wasn't the best idea for keeping up with my training,* I thought as I gulped the water down. I was now wide awake. *Would it be safe to swim in the bay in the rain? Probably not.*

The tide would be going out, and the currents...

Maybe that's what the dream was about—my subconscious warning me about going out in the water while it was raining?

It was definitely possible.

I never understood the nightmares. I wasn't afraid of the open water. Sure, there were predators but there were predators everywhere. If not the animal kind, there were certainly human ones.

And I'd never been afraid to swim in a river or a lake.

There was no such thing as mermaids or mermen. That nightmare was definitely a product of my environment. Mermaids were everywhere in this place.

Little wonder I'd dreamed of a predatory merman trying to lure me to my death.

Shivering in the predawn cold, I grabbed my sweatpants and a sweatshirt out of a drawer. I slipped them on before sitting down at the little desk. I opened my laptop. I didn't have any new e-mails. Dad hadn't answered me, but he wasn't so big on checking e-mail. He usually only did it in the morning before he went to work. He rarely was on the computer other than that, and he didn't have a smartphone, thinking they were a ridiculous waste of money. I went to my Facebook page. I scrolled through the News Feed. It didn't take long for me to get bored.

Honestly, who cared what someone else had for dinner or what someone thinks about a television show?

I closed that tab and opened a new one just as lightning lit up my room. It was so close I could smell ozone. The hair on the back of my neck stood up a bit. It was followed by a blast of thunder so loud and long I wondered if it was going to ever end. The thunder made the windows rattle. Finally it died away. I wasn't used to being this far up in the air during a storm—ever, really. Our house back in Corinth was one story. Storms there never bothered me, but this one seemed to be putting me on edge.

*You're just still on edge because of that weird dream,* I reassured myself as I pulled up a weather site. I typed in the zip code for Latona. The forecast was for rain until at least Saturday morning, but it looked like the thunderstorms would move past by dawn. That was a relief but wasn't good for my swim practice. I drummed my fingers on the desktop. *Maybe I should have stayed in Corinth and worked for Dad all summer again.* I leaned back in the chair.

I hated the very idea of not being able to get in the water.

I did a quick search and confirmed what Joe and Cecily had said over dinner—there didn't seem to be any indoor pool in town. There wasn't even a public outdoor pool—but why would they need one, when people could go to the beach and swim in the bay? The only pool the search engine could find was the Latona Country Club's. If it was anything like the country club in Corinth, I doubted they'd be much interested in letting me use theirs for swim practice, even on a rainy day when the rich girls wouldn't be congregating there in their bikinis and working on their tans. The point of a country club, like my dad always said, was so that people who could afford to join didn't have to mix with people like me.

*I can always go for a jog, and I could go check out that gym,* I thought. I never minded running in the rain. Another flash of lightning was followed by yet another long, low roll of thunder.

I did a search for Latona newspapers, which led me to the site for the *Latona Daily News.* The site was free, so I hesitated just a moment before typing *"Zach Patterson"* into the search engine. The little wheel spun for a few moments, and then a listing of articles came up. I clicked on the first one. It was dated July 26th of last year.

### Lifeguard Missing

Zachary Alan Patterson, 18, of Montgomery, Alabama, was reported missing this morning by his employer, Joseph Hampton, owner and proprietor of Mermaid Inn on the Shore Road. Zachary was last seen at eight p.m. on Friday evening, when he walked out the front door of the Inn. He told Hampton he was planning on walking into town to get something to eat and catch a late movie. Hampton grew concerned Saturday morning when Patterson didn't show up for his lifeguarding shift on the beach. Using a master key to get into Patterson's apartment, Hampton discovered that Patterson's bed had not been slept in. Concerned, he began making calls, trying to locate Patterson. Patterson's car was still in the parking lot at Mermaid Inn. Saturday evening when Patterson still had not turned up, an official missing persons alert was filed with the local police department.

"I didn't think anything of him walking into town rather than driving," Hampton said. "He had a scholarship for swimming to the University of Alabama this fall, and he liked to exercise. He frequently walked into town to run errands rather than driving. I'm just worried there might have been an accident or something, like a hit-and-run or something. He's a good kid."

Patterson's car is still parked at Mermaid Inn, and his belongings are still in his apartment.

He was last seen wearing a white tank top, long khaki shorts and leather sandals.

If anyone has seen Patterson since eight p.m. on Friday evening, or has any information about him, please contact the Latona police department.


There was a photo with the short article. It looked like his senior picture from a high school yearbook. Zach Patterson had white-blond hair he wore cropped very short on the sides, and longer on the top. It was gelled to the center so it stood up a little. He had a slight gap between his front two teeth, but his smile was big and warm. It lit up his face. He was pretty good-looking. His face was symmetrical if a bit round. His eyes were blue, and the yellow sweater he was wearing set off his golden tan. His shoulders looked broad, and the pushed-up sweater sleeves showed strong, muscular forearms.

He didn't look like he had a care in the world.

*What happened to you?* I mused, scrutinizing the picture.

I clicked back to the list. I quickly scanned through the other articles, none of which had anything to add to the original report. His parents had offered a reward, but no one came forward to claim it.

There were some follow-up pieces to the original reports, but they added nothing.

No one in Latona admitted to seeing him that night.

Zach Patterson had walked out the front door of Mermaid Inn and disappeared into thin air.

*The Native Americans thought the mermaids demanded human sacrifice.*

"There's no such thing as mermaids," I said aloud to the rain. "My nightmares are just nightmares."

It was still creepy, though. How does someone just disappear into thin air like that?

I yawned, stretching my arms up and out. My back cracked in a few places. I closed the computer. I climbed back into bed and fell back asleep almost immediately to the soothing sound of the rain hitting the roof.

My phone alarm woke me at precisely six a.m.

It was still raining, so I turned it off and rolled back over.

When I opened my eyes again, it was almost eight in the morning. It was still raining, but it was much brighter outside my windows than it had been in the middle of the night. I yawned, stretched, and got out of bed. I walked into the kitchenette, starting the coffee and putting some bread into the toaster. I went into the bathroom and brushed my teeth. After eating some breakfast, I changed into a tank top and shorts. I decided to go ahead and go for a jog in the rain.

It's not like I was going to melt or anything.

*But you might disappear.*

The rain wasn't coming down very hard as I walked out the front of the Inn. It was really little more than a light sprinkle. I had glanced into the registration office on my way out, but no one was in there. I stepped out onto the veranda and squinted out into the rain. I put on my baseball cap and stretched out before going down the steps. The same cars were parked out there as yesterday. I took a deep breath and started jogging. I ran down the empty parking lot at a slow but steady pace. I made sure no cars were coming before starting to jog down the state road on the gravel shoulder. No cars passed me as I headed in the direction of Latona. I was breathing a bit harder by the time I reached the city limits sign, but my muscles weren't tired so I kept on running. The town was just starting to come to life as I headed down the main drag. I could smell food cooking at the diner as I went past. Some cars were idling in the McDonald's drive through. I kept going, deciding to keep going until I got to Rocky's Auto Repair. There I'd turn back and go up that side road to see if I could find Bayside Fitness.

I was pretty pleased with my breathing. *I'm still in pretty good shape,* I thought as I went through the intersection with the light just before the Piggly Wiggly and Rocky's. My socks were soaked through from splashing through puddles. My clothes were damp but not too bad, clinging to me like cotton skin. The rain was more of a mist now, even though the sky was still filled with dark clouds. I crossed the road when I got to Rocky's. I took a break, standing in the entry to their parking lot and stretching, taking deep breaths. I was about to start running again when someone called my name.

I smiled and waved at Dane. I jogged over to where he was standing in one of the open bays, just out of the rain.

"Are you crazy?" He was wearing cleaner jeans than yesterday and another black tank top. His arms were folded in front of his chest, a cigarette dangling from his lips as he leaned against the wall.

"It's not that bad out here," I replied, watching as he shifted a bit, making his muscles flex. *Is he flirting with me?* I wondered.

"Are you crazy?" he repeated, a bemused smirk on his face. "Don't you have the sense to come in out of the rain?" He shook his head and flicked the cigarette out into the parking lot. He blew the smoke out through his nostrils.

I stepped out of the rain so I was standing next to him inside the garage. I took off my baseball cap and shook it. Water sprayed off in every direction.

"Watch it," he said, taking a step back. "Why you out running in the rain, anyway?"

I shrugged. "Can't swim today, so I figured I'd jog for a while. Gotta get some exercise whenever I can." I glanced up at the sky. "I hate missing out on a swimming workout. Don't want my muscles to get rusty."

He stared at me as if trying to decide whether I was crazy or not. He closed his eyes and sighed. "You're a swimmer. Of course. All lifeguards are swimmers. So water don't bug you, does it?"

"Nope. Not at all. I'd go out and swim in the bay in this if I wasn't worried about currents."

He shook his head. "Crazy. I don't like the water. Too many predators."

"You never go in the bay?"

"No way, not me." He shuddered.

"Are there sharks in the bay?"

"Never heard of any—there haven't been any attacks or anything, but there's other things besides sharks, you know." His shoulders went up and down. He shook another cigarette out of a crumpled pack and lit it, flicking the match out into the parking lot. "I've never liked the water, even when I was a kid. I don't even like to go out on boats."

"But you live on the coast."

He gave me a lazy look. "Yeah, well." His voice took on a wistful tone. "One of these days, I'm going to get out of here. Put Latona in the rearview mirror and never look back, you know? I'm saving my money and moving to New Orleans when I get enough."

"What are you going to do there?"

His eyes narrowed. "When you can work on cars, you can always get work somewhere. I'm going to get the hell out of this little pissant town and never come back."

"Why New Orleans?"

"You ever been?" he asked.

"No, never. Have you?"

"It's like heaven. I got a cousin who lives there." His eyes got dreamy. "Nobody there gives two shits, you know? You mind your own business and everyone else minds theirs. You can be whatever you want, do whatever you want and no one cares as long as you aren't hurting someone else."

"Sounds cool."

"It is." He scowled. "It's not like here, where you can't fart without everyone knowing about it in five goddamned minutes. I hate this place."

"Seems nice enough to me."

"Yeah, well, you ain't from here, either." His eyes glinted. "Where did you say you were from, Corinth?"

"Yeah, Corinth. It's about forty minutes from Tuscaloosa." I nodded. "Come to think of it, I don't much like my hometown either. That's why I'm here for the summer. I couldn't get away from there fast enough." I laughed. "You're right—everyone there knows everyone's business. And people make up their minds about who you are based on who your family is and there's nothing you can do to change their minds."

Our eyes met for a beat too long before he looked away.

"You said you knew that lifeguard who disappeared last summer?" I asked. "Zach Patterson?"

"Yeah. Yeah, I knew him. We hung out a few times." He turned and leaned his back against the wall. "So what?"

I shrugged. "I looked him up online. You think he drowned, right?"

"I don't know." He shrugged again. "Maybe he just got bored hanging around here all summer and bugged out, headed over to

New Orleans or Pensacola or somewhere." He laughed. "People don't want to be found usually don't get found, you know?"

"But wouldn't he have told his parents? That seems weird, doesn't it?"

He looked at me for a long time before answering. "Maybe that's who he wanted to get away from most of all." He laughed. "I don't know what he was doing lifeguarding, anyway. He was a rich kid, you know, from Montgomery. His daddy was a lawyer or something. He went to private school. So what's a kid like that doing down here, lifeguarding for a summer job?" He winked. "I'll tell you what he was doing—he wanted to get away from his parents, that's what. A free summer away from Mom and Dad, out from under their roof and their thumb." He rubbed his chin. "They made him out to be some kind of perfect kid, you know? He wasn't perfect."

"Nobody is."

"Yeah. There was a lot more to Zach Patterson than his parents knew. Their big mistake was letting him come down here for the summer. Because once he tasted freedom, he didn't want to go back to them. I don't blame him…if I could get away from mine you can bet your ass I wouldn't have to think twice about it." He smiled at me lazily. "I need to get back to work. Have a nice run back. Give me a call if you get bored."

## CHAPTER FIVE

It started sprinkling again as I ran up Oak Street. The street sloped slightly upward, so I adjusted my stride. I had gone a block or so when I saw the sign for Bayside Fitness just ahead and to my left. The gym was a long, narrow storefront type building, with a large parking lot. Half of the front was enormous tinted plate-glass windows. A neon *Open* sign was on over the front door. There were a few cars in the parking lot, all grouped together in the spaces by the front door. It stopped raining again as I crossed the road and jogged into the parking lot. The parking lot was potholed, weeds poking up through cracks. Puddles had formed in the potholes and in other places where the uneven pavement was low. I jumped onto the raised sidewalk that ran the length of the building's front. I pushed the door open and stepped inside. The intense cold inside made me shiver, with my wet clothes and skin. I just stood there on a rubber mat as my clothes dripped water.

The building was a lot deeper than it had looked from the outside. I shivered as I took it all in. Racks of weights, benches, weight machines, stationary bikes, treadmills, and elliptical machines were all spread out. The walls were mirrored. A woman in shorts and a sports bra dripped with sweat as she worked on a stair climber. A muscular man in his early thirties groaned and grunted as he did squats. It smelled of bleach and cleaners. The floor was covered with rubber mats, beyond the tiled floor in front of the counter on my right.

"You look like you drowned," the man behind the counter said with a laugh. He was about my height, maybe an inch or two shorter. His blondish-brown hair was cut close to the scalp in a buzz cut. His eyes were a bright blue and he was tan. He was wearing a blue muscle shirt. It clung to the enormous muscles of his chest, and his huge shoulders and arms were road mapped with bulging blue veins. There were wrinkles around his eyes and mouth. His stomach was flat. He was leaning on the counter, drinking a protein shake. It took a few moments for me to realize that his left eye was blackened and swollen, and there was a red blood spot on the white of it. "Here, dry yourself off before you catch cold." He tossed me a fluffy white towel. "What can I do for you?" he asked as I caught the towel. It was warm and smelled like Downy.

"Thanks," I replied, drying off my arms and bending at the waist to towel the water off my legs. "Sorry to be dripping everywhere."

"Eh, no worries. People'll be tracking water in all damned day." He shrugged. "That's why I'm keeping a mop handy." He was staring at me. "You're in pretty good shape. You must be new in town."

"Yeah, I'm here for the summer." I tossed the towel back to him. He caught it and tossed it into an open laundry hamper. "Lifeguarding out at Mermaid Inn. Can I join just for the summer?"

He didn't say anything for a moment or two, just kept watching me without changing his expression. Finally, he said, "Yeah. Be ninety bucks." His voice wasn't nearly as friendly as before. "Three months for ninety bucks. That's a good deal, you know. It's usually forty-five per month. But you pay up front, I'll give you a break, okay?" He stuck out his big calloused hand. I stepped closer so I could shake it. He gripped my hand hard. Not hard enough to hurt, but hard enough to let me know how strong he was.

He was really strong.

"My name's Micah."

"Ricky," I replied. He got out a form and he put it on a clipboard. He pushed the clipboard and a pen across the counter at me.

"Fill that out and then I'll give you the tour," he said, turning away from me and picking up the hamper. The thickly defined muscles in his back rippled. "I need to put this load of towels in the washer. Be back in a sec." He disappeared through a door as I started filling out the paperwork. It was all basic stuff—name, address, phone number, who to contact in an emergency, blah-blah-blah. He came back out just as I finished filling it out. I signed and dated the bottom. He took it from me and moved over to the computer. "You gonna pay cash or charge?"

"I don't have my wallet," I said. "I can't pay now. I can come back later today, though. I want to do some lifting."

"Okay, no problem. I'll just get everything entered in here and log in the fee." He didn't look at me as he typed with his index fingers slowly, frowning at the computer screen. "You can pay the next time you come in. Everyone gets a free workout to start off with anyway. You can go ahead and work out after the tour, if you want." It seemed to take forever, but he finally finished. He opened a drawer and handed me a little tag for my key ring. He waved it in front of the gun mounted on the counter, which beeped and a green light flashed. "You need to swipe that every time you come in, otherwise the insurance won't cover you if you get hurt or drop a weight on your foot or something. You come in and don't swipe the card, I'll cancel your membership, and no refunds, buddy. I don't want no hassles with the insurance bloodsuckers." He peered at me. "You want to change out of them wet clothes? I have some sweats and T-shirts people have left behind—they've been washed so you don't have to worry about that." He grinned. "And I'll wash them again after you wear 'em."

"Thanks, that'd be great." I was still shivering in the air conditioning. It had to be at least thirty degrees colder inside than it was outside. My teeth were close to chattering.

He rummaged around behind the counter in a big box and handed me a pair of navy blue sweatpants and a black T-shirt. He gestured to a door that said *Men* on it. He pushed a pair of flip-flops across the counter at me. "Go on in the locker room and change. Give me your clothes and I'll run them through the dryer for you— if you want to work out, that is. If not, you can just bring that stuff back with you the next time you come in." He shrugged, the muscles in his shoulder caps flexing under the tanned skin like ropes. "Up to you. People who join for a year get a few free training sessions with me, but you don't look like you need a trainer. Do you?"

"I've got a workout already mapped out," I replied. "I'll just stick with that."

"That's what I figured—but if you need a spotter don't hesitate to ask me, you hear? I'd rather you bothered me than you hurt yourself. Bayside Fitness is all about safety. Now go on and get changed so I can give you the tour"—he laughed—"such as it is."

The locker room smelled like all locker rooms do. A strong aroma of sweat barely covered by a liberal dose of pine spray. It was long and narrow. The floor was carpeted—a dark blue indoor-outdoor style. The carpeting ended in white tile at the far side. I could see shower stalls up against the back wall. I walked down there. There were urinals on one wall. The toilet stalls were on the opposite wall. There was another door next to the toilet stalls that was almost all glass. There were a couple of dials on the wall next to the door. I assumed it was either a steam room or a sauna. I walked back to the main part where lockers were lined up on opposing walls. There were both upper and lower lockers. Some of them had combination locks on the handles. There was a shelf with fluffy white towels stacked neatly in double rows. Beneath was a laundry hamper with a laminated sign just above reading: DO NOT STEAL OUR TOWELS! THIS MEANS YOU!

On the wall above the lockers on the right side were framed and autographed photos of bodybuilders. But on the opposite wall the photos were all of Micah. Some of them showed him standing in the middle of a wrestling ring wearing skimpy blue trunks, soaked in sweat, flexing his arms with his foot up on another prone man. There were also a couple of portraits of him with a championship belt around his waist, hands on his hips, every muscle in his body flexing. There was a smug smile on his tanned face. He looked younger in the pictures, like he was in his twenties or early thirties when they were taken. His hair was longer, framing his face with golden curls. The hair underneath the curls was darker. Still blond, but it was a lot darker than the curls. His oiled muscles gleamed. Veins popped out. He was still in great shape, but the combination of youth and physical perfection in the photos was almost breathtaking.

*I bet he got laid a lot back then.* I pulled my shirt over my head. *Then again, he probably still does. He's in great shape.*

I sat on one of the benches and untied my shoes. After taking off my socks, I shook them out a bit and placed them on top of my folded shirt. My shorts and underwear came off next, and I folded them neatly on the pile. I pulled up the sweatpants and slipped the T-shirt on over my head. It was a little too small, pulling tightly across my back and chest. It also exposed about an inch of skin above the waistband of the sweatpants. *It'll have to do,* I thought as I slipped my feet into the flip-flops and picked up the pile of clothes. I glanced at the framed photo next to the door. Micah was posing with his right side to the camera, every glistening muscle flexed. There was a tattoo on his upper arm. I leaned in to get a better look.

*It was a merman.*

I swallowed and walked back out to the counter.

"Thanks for drying these," I said as I handed my clothes over to Micah.

He smiled at me lazily. "Not a problem." He disappeared through the door again after giving me yet another appraising look up and down. When he came back out, he flipped up a section of the counter and walked through. He gestured for me to follow him.

"Obviously, this is the weight room." He took me around, showing me all the machines and benches and other contraptions. He kept a steady patter. I gathered it was his standard sales pitch for prospective new members. I didn't need to be sold on buying a membership, but I gathered he didn't have another spiel. He explained how each machine worked, even though I already knew, and what they were for. There were several racks with dumbbells facing a mirrored wall. He picked the pair of thirty pounders and demonstrated a couple of exercises for me. I think he was just looking to show off and pump up his impressive muscles more than anything else.

There was also a cardio room. The floor inside was padded, and hand weights were stacked in a corner next to several stacks of steps. A class schedule was posted on the door. He showed me the row of cardio machines along one wall, treadmills and stair climbers and bicycles and elliptical machines. He led me to another door, smiled at me, and said, "This is the big surprise—the one thing you won't find at any other gym, either here in town or anywhere else in the country." His chest puffed up with pride. His smile was dazzling, proud. He paused for a moment before throwing the door open. He stepped inside and flipped a switch. He stood just inside the door and gave me room so I could walk inside past him.

"Wow," I said, not really sure what else to say.

There was a ring set up in the center of the room, which had a really high ceiling. The floor around the ring was padded. The walls were mirrored. There were mats spread out on one side of the room. A couple of punching bags hung on chains from the ceiling. In one corner, a couple of speed bags dangled.

"A ring? Wow," I said, walking over to the side of it. The floor of the ring was navy blue. In the very center in large yellow letters were the initials *ML*. "What do the letters stand for?"

"My ring name was Micah Lightning." He smiled proudly. "When I first got started in the ring when I was eighteen, they called me the Lightning Bolt, or Kid Lightning. When I got older, I changed it to Micah Lightning."

"I saw the pictures in the locker room. How long were you a pro wrestler?" I tested the bottom rope by pulling on it. It had a little give but was pretty taut.

"I retired from the ring when I was about thirty-one. That's when I opened this place. Had to have a ring, though." He looked pleased at my interest. "I was a big deal too. I was a champion, and the fans loved me." He flexed his big biceps. "I had to give it up when I hurt my back. I could still get in the ring and wrestle, but I had to be careful. And if you're not going to give them one hundred and ten percent effort to put on a good show, you're not worth a bag of popcorn to the promotion." He shook his head sadly. His deep blue eyes took on a dreamy look. "And when you hold back is when you're more likely to get hurt, you know? So I retired, gave it up." He shrugged nonchalantly. "I sometimes get in the ring and show people some moves. You've got a pretty good build, nice and lean and muscular. And tall. You ever think about being a pro wrestler? I could train you. I wouldn't charge you for it—I just love to get in the ring and work out, still." He pointed at his black eye. "I know you've been wondering about this. I'm training a local kid who has a lot of potential. Sometimes you make mistakes and people get hurt."

"Ah."

"You really should give it a try. It's fun and you can make some decent money."

I shook my head. "I'm a swimmer. Got a scholarship to Bama." I cracked a smile. "I'm not very coordinated. I'm more at home in the water."

The smile on his face faded. "Mermaid Inn's lifeguard last summer had a scholarship to Bama too." His voice was a monotone, expressionless.

"Yeah, I've heard about him," I replied. "Did you know him? Did he work out here?"

"Yeah, he worked out here, before he disappeared." He gave a little shrug. "It's either here or the Y, and the Y hasn't gotten new equipment since Eisenhower was president. They don't have a pool, before you ask. The only places to swim around here are the bay or the river, and I wouldn't recommend the river. There's gators in the river." He switched off the light and ushered me back out into the weight room. "Yeah, he got in the ring with me a couple of times. I didn't know him well—he just wanted to see what it was like. He had potential too, but he said he was more of a swimmer than anything else. Just wanted to have the experience, he said. He seemed like a good kid." He shook his head. "A shame."

"It seems weird that he'd disappear that way." I climbed up on the ring's apron. "I mean, to walk away from his job and his family?"

"He sure left the Hamptons in the lurch. Didn't seem like that kind of kid, but that just goes to show you don't know what someone's like, do you?"

"So he just left? Maybe it wasn't voluntary."

"Police didn't find any evidence of any hanky-panky." He shrugged and snapped his fingers. "Disappeared right into thin air."

"Maybe I should be careful." I jumped back down to the matted floor. "If Mermaid Inn lifeguards tend to disappear…"

He laughed. "Well, you're only the second lifeguard they've had. I don't know if one disappearance counts as a trend."

"Really?"

He nodded. "Two years ago a couple of kids staying there drowned in the bay. It was weird—their bodies never washed ashore. Their parents both fell asleep on the beach, and the last thing they remembered was their boys were out swimming in the water. When they woke up the kids weren't around. The Coast Guard dragged the bay and everything. Nothing." He snapped his fingers. "It was quite a story around here, you can imagine. So that fall, the city council passed an ordinance that any public place with a beach had to have a lifeguard during the summer season. That Zach kid was the first one the Hamptons hired. That's why his running off left them in such a lurch. They couldn't let people down on the beach without a lifeguard. They finally had to hire some guy from Mobile who commuted for the rest of the summer. Cost them an arm and a leg too."

"That sucks."

He laughed. "Yeah, well"—he made a face at me—"be careful when you're out in the water or the mermaids will get you."

"Mermaids?"

He waved a hand. "It's how the place got its name, some stupid old legends about mermaids living in the bay. I've never seen one, and I've been here my whole life."

I bit my lower lip. "I noticed in one of your pictures in the locker room you have a merman tattoo?"

He smirked and rolled up his right shirtsleeve, exposing a tattoo very similar to Dane's. He flexed the muscle so the tail moved around a bit. "I got this when I was wrestling."

"Because you're from Mermaid Bay?"

"I don't remember. It seemed like a good idea at the time." He rolled the shirtsleeve back down. "You going to go ahead and work out now?"

"I think I'll come back later," I replied. "Think I should probably head back out to the Inn now."

He handed me a battered-looking umbrella. "Here. Someone left this here, unless you're going to run."

"Thanks." My body had cooled down, and my legs felt tired. "I think I'll just walk back."

I stepped outside. The rain was coming down a lot harder than it had been before. I opened the umbrella. It was a small one, but it would at least keep my head from getting wet.

I'd passed the library on the way to the gym and decided to stop in on my way back to the Inn. It was about a block closer to the bay than the gym. I carefully stepped around puddles and walked up the sidewalk to the Latona Public Library. It was a neat, compact two-story brick building. I climbed the steps to the porch, closing the umbrella and shaking off the excess water. I opened the door and went in. It was cold inside, the air conditioning blasting so hard it felt like it was probably about fifty degrees inside. I was shivering as I walked up to the front desk.

The young woman working there didn't look like she was very much older than me. She was pretty, carrying a little bit of extra weight, but she wore it well. She had reddish-blond hair pulled back from her pretty face. Her face appeared to be all angles—sharp chin, small forehead, protruding cheekbones. There were freckles scattered over her white skin. She had thin eyebrows plucked into arches above her round dark brown eyes. She was wearing a white blouse over a khaki skirt that dropped to around her knees. She was scanning a pile of books with a wand. The wand beeped as she held it up to the lower spine of a red book without a dust jacket. She looked at the computer screen before placing it on the cart just behind the counter. Her wire-framed glasses were at the bottom of her nose.

She pushed them up. "What can I help you with?"

"Hi. I'm spending the summer here, and I'd like to get a library card."

"Are you a resident of Alabama?" When I nodded, she smiled. "If you have a library card from your town, I can issue you one for our library." She looked at me over the top of her glasses. "You must be the new lifeguard up at Mermaid Inn."

As I started to say something, she waved her hand. "We don't get a lot of strangers around here, so the ones we do tend to stand out. Joe told me the lifeguard was arriving yesterday, and you look like a swimmer to me." She held out her hand. "My name is Margery Lippman."

"Ricky Hackworth." I shook her small, warm hand. "Nice to meet you."

"Welcome to Latona. Hackworth, you said?" Her smile was genuine and warm. She turned back to the computer and started typing. "Where are you from?"

"Corinth."

Her fingers kept flying over the keyboard. "And there you are. No overdue fines, so I don't see a problem. If you'll just give me a second…" She retrieved a card from one of the desk drawers, wrote my name on the front of it, and attached a bar code sticker to the back. She handed it to me with a flourish. "And there you are. Is there anything I can help you with?"

"I was just at the gym—Bayside Fitness—and the owner said something interesting." I smiled as she rolled her eyes.

"Micah Gaylord never said anything interesting in his life," she replied flatly. "He traded his brains for muscles long before you were born." She tapped her fingernails on the counter and shook her head. "Sorry, that was mean. What did he say?"

"He said something about how there's some legend about the bay—about mermaids?"

"Merfolk." She bit her lower lip and smiled. "Yes, that's our local legend, going back to Native American times, and it's also how the bay got its name. And Mermaid Inn. Have you seen the mermaid statue down at the waterfront?"

I shook my head. "No, I haven't."

"It's Latona's pride and joy." She laughed. "When the French first discovered Mobile Bay, the natives warned them against coming to this bay. The natives said that creatures that were half fish and half human lived here in the water. They demanded human sacrifice, and preyed on humans. If residents of the community didn't send a young man out in a canoe every summer to feed the fish people, they would send a powerful storm. The French didn't believe them, of course, and sent an expedition down here from the settlement up at Mobile to explore and chart the area. No one ever saw the expedition again." She laughed. "I know it sounds crazy, but there you go. The French steered clear of this part of the state until the Spanish took over, and they ignored the Indians and some of them disappeared too." She frowned. "They called this place *La Sirena*. But after the War of 1812, Americans settled here without any problems. Every once in a while someone disappears, or someone thinks they see a mermaid out there in the bay, but it's all nonsense. There's no such thing as mermaids. But that's why it's called Mermaid Bay." She leaned over the counter. "The story is the mermaids protect us from hurricanes—we never get it as bad here as the rest of the bay and the Gulf Coast does, you know. We never get a direct hit, and the storm surge isn't as bad here as it gets everywhere else."

"How can that be possible?"

"There's bound to be an explanation for it that doesn't involve mermaids. I don't know. Maybe the storms drive the water up Mobile Bay and we just get spillover. I don't know. But there are some people around here who believe the old stories to this day." She brushed a stray strand of hair out of her face. "You know what *Latona* is?"

GREG HERREN

"No, ma'am."

"Latona is another name for Leto."

"Leto?"

"In Greek mythology she was the mother of Apollo and Artemis, god of the sun and goddess of the moon." She smiled. "Zeus appeared to her in the form of a swan and impregnated her with the twins."

"She had sex with a swan?" I made a face. "That's just weird."

"There's a lot of bestiality in Greek mythology—Zeus was always turning himself into some kind of animal to seduce women. It's kind of creepy, now that you mention it," she replied solemnly. "So, you're interested in our local legends and local history? Today's your lucky day." She turned to the cart behind her, stacked high with books. She took one off the top and handed it to me. "There you are."

It was the red book with no dust jacket she'd just put on the cart, so I turned it and looked at the spine. "*Mermaids and Magic: A History of Latona, Alabama*," I read aloud. "By Nathan Ricker."

"You want to read it?" She smiled at me. When I nodded, she took it back from me. She scanned the bar code on the back of my new library card, then the bar code at the bottom of the spine. "There." She pushed the book back into my hands. "It's due back in two weeks. You'll get a reminder e-mail two days before it's due. It's actually a pretty interesting book," she said as I opened it to the first page. "Dr. Ricker, the author, actually lives farther up the road from Mermaid Inn. He did a really good job of collecting the legends about the bay—and researching the actual history."

"Cool." I put the book under my arm. "Did you know the lifeguard from last summer? Zach Patterson?"

She bit her lower lip. "I knew who he was, and of course, after he disappeared…but no, I never met him. Why?"

"Well, I was just thinking, what with the legends and everything…"

She rolled her eyes. "You aren't thinking the mermaids took him?"

I could feel my face coloring as I nodded. "I mean, it makes sort of sense."

She laughed. "No, Ricky, the mermaids didn't get Zach. That boy just took off, or something happened to him, but whatever it was, it wasn't the mermaids."

"Crazy, right?" I smiled back and waved the book at her. "Thanks for this."

"If you need anything else, you just let me know. The library's not open on Sundays and Mondays, but I'm here from eleven to seven every other day." She hesitated for a moment, then continued, "Latona may seem unfriendly at first, but it's really a nice place. I hope you enjoy your stay here."

"I'm sure I will." I turned and walked back outside.

# CHAPTER SIX

I had trouble sleeping that night.

I had the worst dreams ever.

I went to bed around ten, hoping to get a good night's rest before spending the next day dehydrating in the summer heat and watching the swimmers, ready to leap into action at the first sign of trouble. As soon as I closed my eyes, I drifted off to sleep—

—and was adrift in the hot sun, floating on a raft. The bay was completely calm, no waves, no wind, not even a wisp of a cloud in the vast blue sky overhead. On the shore behind me, a group of Native Americans holding torches were chanting something as I drifted farther and farther away from the shore. A drum was beating in time with the chanting.

*There's no such thing as mermaids,* I told myself, *this whole thing is ridiculous, virgin sacrifices to mermaids for protection from the storms, it's crazy, none of this makes any sense.*

And something hit the raft from underneath, tilting it, and even though I scrabbled desperately for a handhold, I slid off into the warm blue water.

My head went under the water, but I kicked strongly with my legs and my head broke the surface. Panting, I sucked in air and looked around for the raft.

It was gone, like it had never been there.

I could feel the terror rising in me.

A large fin broke the surface near me, and I screamed, trying to swim back to shore.

Something grabbed my foot and dragged me back under.

A male face, pale and bluish with crazed blue eyes was just inches from mine. He opened his mouth and I could see the sharp teeth, the fangs, and somehow I knew, even though I really couldn't hear, he was laughing, laughing maniacally with glee and joy as another form swam around us, long hair floating behind in the water, and his hand came up, and his nails were long and clawed, and he raked them down my front, and blood, blood was everywhere, and the pain was so intense, the worst pain I'd ever felt, and I opened my mouth and screamed—

I sat up in my bed, panting and gasping.

Thunder roared, almost like it was just outside my window. The wind was howling and rain was pelting the roof. The entire building seemed to be shaking, the gable window rattling like the wind was trying to get inside, trying to get to me. I heard some odd noise out on the roof, like scrabbling of some kind, like claws on the tiles, and I felt the scream of terror rising in my throat. I climbed out of the bed, terrified, looking out the window, and there was something out there, something that was coming for me…

I turned and ran. I unlocked my door and could hear weird sounds from out in the hallway, wet sloshing sounds. I opened the door, saying a prayer under my breath, and I could hear the squeaking of the dumbwaiter as it rose through the house in its shaft.

Instinctively I knew whatever was in the dumbwaiter wanted me.

Just like the thing on the roof.

I ran for the stairs, pulling the door open and heading down the narrow steps, barely able to breathe the air was so heavy and stifling hot, sweat gushing from my pores like mini-fountains, but it was a cold sweat, the cold sweat of absolute terror as I flew down the stairs, and I could hear something coming down the stairs behind me, something wet and angry and—

*Hungry.*

Lightning lit up the third floor as I burst out of the third-floor door and ran for the next staircase. I could hear it coming. The house shook with the thunder, but when I reached the top of the stairs something was coming up the stairs.

It was wet, leaving puddles behind as it came up the stairs, the pale skin, the legs covered with blue scales, and it looked up, the long wet hair falling away from the face as he bared his sharp teeth at me in a grin...

I turned, but another one was coming out of the staircase door I'd just come through.

There was nowhere for me to go.

As they closed in on me, I could see the merman tattoos on their upper arms.

I sat up in bed, gasping.

I looked at the nightstand clock. It was a few minutes before six. I reached over and turned off the alarm—no need for it since I was already awake. The sun wasn't up yet, the sky through the window still various shades of dark blue and purple. I yawned and sat up, blinking when I switched on the bedside lamp as my eyes adjusted.

*Damn, those were some intense dreams,* I thought as I flipped the coffeemaker switch on, having gotten it ready before going to bed. I went into the bathroom for my usual morning routine. My pulse was still racing. I splashed cold water in my face and stared at my reflection. *There's no such thing as mermaids,* I reassured myself. *Is it any wonder you had bad dreams after yesterday?*

It had all seemed so real, though.

I shivered again as the adrenaline began to die away.

*Maybe I should skip my morning swim.*

"You're being stupid," I scolded the mirror. "It was just a fucking dream."

Teeth, wash the face, gargle. I tossed some bread in the toaster and gulped down a cup of hot black coffee. I ate some toast and a protein bar, drank down another cup of coffee, and put on my racing trunks. I draped a towel around my neck, slipped my feet into flip-flops, and headed down the stairs in the silent building. The huge old house was dark and quiet. The only sound was the slap of my flip-flops against the floor and the soles of my feet. The sky was turning pink in the distance as I warmed up on the beach, shaking my arms and pinwheeling them, first one way, then the other. I kicked off my flip-flops and hesitated for just a moment before wading out into the dark warm water. My feet sank a little bit into the soft sandy bottom. When the water was up to my thighs I inhaled and dove into it.

The water was dark and mysterious. I could see nothing in the depths beneath me. I pushed the memory of my nightmare aside. There was nothing in the water. There was no such thing as mermen. Predators were attracted by blood or by distressed strokes. As long as I kept my strokes steady, I had nothing to fear from anything out there.

Right, left, right. Taking a deep breath on every left-arm stroke the way I was trained, the way I always did, the same rhythmic movement through the water.

*Put everything aside and focus on your strokes. Each arm into the water smoothly, try not to slap the surface, but rather slide your hand into it. And keep the count so you know when to make your turn and swim back the other way.*

I stayed in the water for two hours. The same workout routine I always followed. I always started with the freestyle stroke. Followed by the backstroke, butterfly, and the breast strokes. Always counting each and every stroke to keep track of the distance traveled. Focus on stroke after stroke, always making sure to breathe fully. Expand the lungs and take in as much oxygen as possible as quickly as I could. Then exhale every bit of oxygen, blowing it out until there was nothing left in my lungs. Ignore the burning sensation in every muscle. Ignore it even as they ache and scream and burn with lactic acid. Stay focused on moving forward, always moving forward until the twentieth stroke when I flipped, to head back the other way. *Keep moving forward even though it hurts, even though every movement makes the muscles burn and ache, even when you think you can't go any further. Ignore your muscles sending messages to your brain begging to stop.* After a while the message was muted and the pain became almost ecstatic. Adrenaline and endorphins mixed in the blood and kept the body going.

I've read about yogis who reach a Zen state through punishment of the body. It's what swimming is for me. The rhythm of the breathing and the movement, the punishing and pushing of my body beyond what it thinks it can stand, send me into a zone as I keep the count going. One…two…three…four…I am always slightly aware of other stimuli. I am aware the sun is rising and that I can see through the water, schools of fish sometimes passing beneath me. Crabs scuttle along the bottom where the water is shallower. The water begins to seem warmer, the sun beats down on my skin. And I keep swimming, I keep counting. I will not stop before I've finished.

I will not quit. I will never give in to the little voice deep inside my brain, begging me to listen to my screaming muscles and stop. *Just this once won't hurt,* the voice pleads as I continue moving through the salty water, *your muscles do need to rest every once in a while. What will it hurt to stop half an hour early, ten minutes, or even just five? You've got speed and endurance already, what will it hurt, wouldn't you rather relax and have something to eat?*

But there is always something else I could do rather than my workout. I could always sleep late. I could always find something to read or something to watch on television, find some way of entertaining myself besides practicing.

But still I push myself, ignoring that inner voice. When my body wants to stop, I keep going. If I give up now, then all the mornings I've gotten up at five were for nothing. Everything I've sacrificed would be meaningless.

Sometimes when I get to the point where every breath burns and every muscle fiber in my body is screaming, I hear things in my head besides the voice. I hear memories, bad memories I've tried to forget.

I hear whispers and laughter. I hear the word *fag* sneered at me in the hallway, in the locker room, at swim meets, and at school.

I could see Dane's tattoo as I swam. I heard him saying *He disappeared, maybe he went to New Orleans.*

I saw Micah's matching tattoo. *Why did they have matching tattoos?*

Sometimes when I swim I close my eyes. Not that morning, not after those dreams. Every so often I thought I saw something moving in the water beneath me and a chill went through me before my rational mind reminded me that it was probably just a fish.

*There's no such thing as mermaids.*

Yet I knew they were down there, waiting for me, watching. I could feel their staring eyes, almost hear their mocking laughter. At any moment I was certain a cold hand would grasp my ankle, too strong for me to resist, dragging me down into the water, the sharp talons and teeth ripping at my flesh, ripping out my throat, feasting on me, I would never be seen again, I would be just another one of the young men who vanished in the bay, part of the legend, the most recent at first, but in future years I'd be forgotten—

I pushed the nightmares aside, and to teach my brain a lesson I did some extra laps.

Finally I was finished. I put my feet down on the bottom. The water was to my waist. I stood there for a moment and just breathed, deep and slow the way I'd been taught from childhood. My skin felt hot. I splashed my way to the shoreline, out of the glassy water. I stood there, shaking out my arms and legs to get the blood flowing. It was just past eight by my waterproof watch and already getting hot. The beach was still deserted, empty. It was like something out of a post-apocalyptic movie. The silence was unnerving. The Inn seemed to be brooding, waiting for something.

If not for the gulls and the occasional mullet breaking the water's surface, the world could have ended while I'd been in the water swimming.

I got the big bottle of water I'd brought out with me. It was lukewarm, but I gulped it down. I wrapped my beach towel around my waist and crossed the sand, the white sugary powder scrunching and squeaking under my bare feet. I climbed the worn gray steps to the wooden walkway over the dunes.

I was sweating by the time I reached the gallery. There was a freestanding shower there, with a drain. There was a sign: *Please rinse off and dry yourself before coming inside. Thank you. Management.*

I draped my towel over the railing and turned the shower on. Methodically I washed the sand off my legs and the salt from my skin. The water was cold and it felt good. I opened my mouth and drank directly from the stream from the showerhead. I let the water wash over me, closing my eyes.

And again heard the squeak of the dumbwaiter.

"It was a bad dream," I repeated the mantra again. "It never happened, it was just a bad dream."

I turned off the water and toweled myself dry before going inside, wrapping the towel around my waist again—I felt pretty sure Cecily didn't want to see me in my racing suit. But I didn't see anyone as I climbed the steps on my exhausted legs. I unlocked my door and grabbed a protein shake out of the refrigerator. I drank it and another bottle of water before I lay back down on my bed for a quick nap. The alarm on my phone went off at nine thirty. I took a quick shower to wake me up, drank down another protein drink, and got dressed. I grabbed my waterproof lifeguard bag and slipped one of the straps over my shoulder.

The Inn was silent as I went downstairs and out to the lifeguard tower. The beach was still deserted. I put on my sunglasses and climbed up. Even though I would mostly be shaded all day, I slathered sunscreen on my skin. I crossed my legs and opened my copy of *Mermaids and Magic.* I took a lunch break at one and was back on the tower by one thirty. I drank lots of water and ate protein bars for snacks. I read and occasionally looked up to watch the beach and the water. At six, I climbed down from the tower and went inside for dinner. At eight I was back in the water swimming laps. By ten I was back in my bed, the alarm set for six the next morning.

That became my routine, similar to my routine when I was at home. Sometimes, rather than a morning swim, I got in the truck and drove into the gym to lift weights for an hour and spend another hour alternating between the elliptical, the stationary bike, and the stair climber. One night instead of making something for dinner, I headed into town to the Singing Mermaid for something battered and fried. My timing was off. Alana wasn't working, and I wound up with a tired-looking waitress in her midthirties who chewed gum and kept calling me *hon*.

Micah was never at the gym on the mornings when I stopped in. The place was practically deserted at that hour, other than maybe a couple of women on the ellipticals and the sleepy-looking boy folding towels at the counter. It was fine with me. My time was limited and I'd rather focus on my workout. But it was always a bit of a letdown.

The days passed in monotony. When Tuesday finally rolled around as my first day off, I got up at the usual time. I always find it best to not alter my routine. If I sleep late on my days off, that makes it harder to get up when I have to again. So I got up, swam my laps, and went back to bed. I slept for a few hours before getting up for the day.

I was almost finished with *Mermaids and Magic* and wanted to see if I could find Nathan Ricker. The book was really interesting. There were a lot more legends—and supposedly, mermaid sightings—than anyone had let me know.

The Native Americans did indeed stay away from Mermaid Bay before the Europeans came. The local tribe considered it a cursed place and gave it as wide a berth as possible. Dr. Ricker was unable to find any Native American documentation—all the information he was able to collect about their legends came from their interactions with the French explorers, who did write things down. The story of the lost French expedition was clearly documented, and the French proved to be just as superstitious as the natives. Even a priest blessing Mermaid Bay wasn't enough to convince the French to explore the inlet or settle on its shores.

But the French settlement at Mobile flourished. Mermaid Bay became a base for smugglers and pirates, who had no such fears about curses and mermaids. Dirty Louis, whose father was French and mother a slave on Saint-Domingue, established a small settlement on the shores of Mermaid Bay and made it his base of operations—the French wouldn't come anywhere near the place. Since he primarily preyed upon the Spanish treasure ships heading for Spain from the mines of Mexico and South America, the French left him in peace. Dirty Louis also, Dr. Ricker claimed, paid bribes to the governor—a certain percentage of pirate loot wound up in the governor's coffers. There was a lot of trade between Mobile and Pirate Town, as it was called.

Then, one day, the pirates simply disappeared without a trace. Dirty Louis and his ship, *Queen Marie,* were never seen again— and the town itself was completely deserted. The Native Americans swore it was the sea fish-women.

This history seemed to repeat itself, over and over.

The local natives claimed the fish-people had taken the villagers. After the War of 1812, the Americans settled the town of Latona, the first time people lived on the shores of the bay since the people of Pirate Town vanished. The disappearances continued. During the Civil War, any number of Union sailors went AWOL after the Union Navy captured Mobile. But Dr. Ricker seemed to think the legends were all bullshit. *Men disappear all the time,* he wrote in his conclusion to the book, *and it's not like there aren't sharks in the Gulf waters or alligators in the rivers and bayous that drain into the bay.*

While it was certainly true, it didn't help with my dreams.

Every night as soon as I closed my eyes, I was back in the waters of the bay, swimming desperately to escape pursuers with thickly muscled torsos and fish bodies. Every night I could hear their underwater calls to me, felt the strong hands grasping my legs, felt the teeth and the clawlike fingernails tearing into my body, ripping the skin away from the bone.

Or I was adrift again on the raft, with the chanting natives on the shore with their drums and torches while the merfolk swam around me, teasing me and toying with me, taunting me with the prospect of escape, of getting away, before dumping me into the water and ripping me to pieces.

The Inn itself didn't help matters. I kept imagining I could hear claws on the roof, and the wind rattling my windows made me jump out of my skin. And that damned dumbwaiter. Every time it was used, the squeaking and screeching as it climbed up to the top floor set my teeth on edge. I could never be sure if it wasn't my dream come to life, that there was a merman inside of it coming to kill me.

*You're really turning into a drama queen,* I would tell myself over and over again, as my heart pounded in my chest and my breath came too fast, calming myself down and trying to relax in the creepy old inn.

After eating breakfast on my day off I headed downstairs. There were still no guests checked in, but Joe had told me the Inn was booked full for the coming weekend. There was so much relief in his voice when he said it I had to wonder about his financial situation. The Inn couldn't be cheap to keep up, and the power bill had to be astronomical. It wasn't any of my business, of course, but I did hope I wouldn't have to worry about getting paid. That happened to my dad a few times, and it sucked.

Cecily had been avoiding me ever since they'd had me over for dinner. I didn't really care too much. I stopped caring about whether people liked me or not when I was a kid. I wasn't here to make friends. I was here to work and train. Whether Miss Cecily liked me or not wasn't something I was going to lose sleep over.

But I really wanted to meet Nathan Ricker and talk to him about his book. Margery Lippman had told me he lived near Mermaid Inn. I did a web search for him, but the address was pretty nondescript and didn't show up when I tried to find it on Google Maps. There was also no phone number listed for him. As I went down the main stairs, I was going to ask whichever Hampton was working the front desk. I hoped it wasn't Cecily. Joe was always friendly and nice.

My heart sank when I poked my head in the office to see Cecily sitting there.

She was chewing on a pencil, her eyes fixed on her laptop. She didn't bother to even look up at me. "What do you need?" she asked in a bored voice.

I exhaled and counted to ten. If I didn't need information from her I would have just walked away. "I was wondering if you knew Nathan Ricker."

She paused and looked up. She smirked. "Dr. Ricker? Isn't that interesting. You've read his book, then."

"Yeah, I thought it was interesting. I had some questions I wanted to ask him. So?"

She stared at me, no expression on her face. "Zach wanted to meet him too. Weird the way history seems determined to repeat itself." She turned back to her laptop. "You planning on disappearing too?"

"I'll let you know."

That startled her. She whipped her head back around and stared at me, frowning. After a few moments, she grudgingly said, "At the foot of the driveway you turn right, like you're going to town. Just before you get to the city limit sign, there's a gravel road on the left side. That's his driveway."

"Should I call first? Is it okay to just drop in on him?"

"How should I know? I've never met him. He's just a crazy old man. Have fun with that." She turned her eyes back to the laptop, dismissing me.

I decided to walk. The humidity was thick as syrup. My shirt was soaked by the time I got to the bottom of the front steps. I peeled off the wet shirt and tucked it into the back of my shorts. I opened my bottle of water and took a deep swig. By the time I got to the road, my shorts and socks were also soaked through. I put in my earbuds and started walking briskly on the gravel shoulder alongside the pavement. No cars passed in either direction. Heat waves shimmered above the blacktop. I swatted at fleas and mosquitoes, wiped sweat from my forehead and out of my eyes. It took me about fifteen minutes to reach the gravel driveway she'd described. I crossed the road and started walking up the gravel. The foliage was thick, and the pine forest on either side of the driveway was enormous, blocking out the sun. I was grateful for the shade, but the trees also blocked the breeze from the bay. It was like walking in a steam bath.

After about fifty yards the driveway curved around to the left. I went around the curve and a small bungalow came into view. There was an old green Chevrolet parked in front of the screened-in porch. I took a deep breath and finished the water.

As I walked up to the front steps, a voice called out from the shadows inside the porch. "What do you want? I'm not interested in buying anything, so you can just turn around and march yourself right back out of here."

"I'm not selling anything," I yelled back. "I'm looking for Dr. Ricker."

"Why?"

"I'm reading his book about the area and I have some questions."

The screen door opened. A man who looked to be about seventy or so stood in the doorway. He was wearing a Havana hat, khaki shorts, and a University of Florida T-shirt. Wisps of white hair were scattered over his liver-spotted head. His blue eyes were sharp and alert. "Read my book, have you? Clearly, you are an intelligent and discerning young man of great taste." He smiled. "Come on up here on the porch. You want some iced tea?"

"That would be great." I stepped inside and the screen door slammed shut behind me. An orange tabby blinked at me from a wooden chair. A couple of ceiling fans spun and swung overhead. It was very cool on the porch. A breeze was blowing through the rusty-looking screens. I sat down and he poured me a sweaty glass of tea.

"You know who I am. But you are…?"

"Ricky Hackworth." I took a big gulp of the tea. It was perfect. "I'm the lifeguard for the summer over at Mermaid Inn, and Margery at the library recommended your book to me."

"Lifeguard?" He peered at me. "Isn't that odd? Second summer in a row the Mermaid Inn lifeguard has shown up here to talk to me about my book."

That jolted me. "Zach Patterson came by to talk to you?"

He nodded. "Shame he disappeared like that—he was a nice kid, seemed like." He shook his head. "Nobody wants to say it loud, like if no one says it he's still alive, but he is surely dead and buried. Or been fed to the gators in the bayou."

Another jolt. "You don't think he disappeared, then?"

"Why would he?" He poured himself another glass of the tea. "He had everything to live for, a great life—or so it seemed on the surface. None of us ever really knows what kind of demons anyone else is living with, do we? But he seemed like he had it made, everything he could want…Parents who loved him, a nice car, swimming scholarship, young and good looking and intelligent. He would have gone far. No, I've never believed he walked away from his life. Someone killed him, sure as I'm sitting here."

"Did you know him well?"

"Nah, he just came by a couple of times to talk to me about the book, same as you." He peered at me. "Interesting coincidence, don't you think?"

"Yeah," I replied.

"What kind of questions do you have about my book?"

I hesitated. "It's going to sound stupid."

He laughed. "Now, Ricky, I always used to tell my students there are no stupid questions." He peered at me. "It's not true, of course—you wouldn't believe the stupid questions people have asked me—but ask me anything you want about the book." He took off his glasses and rubbed his eyes. "You and the Patterson boy are the only people to show any interest in that old book in a long time. So ask away."

I hesitated before blurting out, "Do you believe the legends?"

He whistled. "You read the book, didn't you? What do you think?"

"You made it pretty clear you didn't."

"I was an academic when I wrote that book," he replied after thinking for a minute or two. "No academic could ever admit to believing in anything supernatural—not if he wants to keep his job." He sighed. "I'm from this area, Ricky. I grew up here. Now, I never saw anything even remotely close to a mermaid in the bay. Not once. But you know, when you start researching things, you can't help but wonder. Of course there's always a logical explanation for everything. Dirty Louis, for example. His ship could have been caught in a hurricane out in the Gulf and sunk—back in those days they had no weather tracking, so hurricanes and tropical storms seemed to just come from out of nowhere. As for Pirate Town, well, there are any number of explanations. A yellow-fever epidemic could have wiped them out. Dirty Louis could have been trying to move them to a new location when the boat sank." He snapped his fingers. "I can think of any number of logical, rational explanations that don't include the vengeance of angry mermaids." He sighed. "But when there is a pattern of strange disappearances…"

"So Zach Patterson was the latest in a history?"

"Worried you'll be next to go?" He polished his glasses with a white handkerchief and looked at me. He shrugged. "Like I said in the book, there's any number of explanations for why people disappear that don't have anything to do with mermaids that eat human flesh." He laughed. "Just saying it sounds crazy, doesn't it?"

"I'm not worried—I don't believe in that kind of stuff, ghosts and all that, but"—I hesitated—"I did have a nightmare the first night I stayed at the Inn. It was about a merman. I've never dreamed anything like that before."

"That could have just been a reaction to being here. Mermaid Bay, Mermaid Inn, the power of suggestion…it's not that strange, really, if you think about it," Dr. Ricker replied. "Stranger things have happened. You don't believe it was some kind of supernatural thing, do you? A warning from another dimension?"

His eyes were twinkling and a smile was twitching at the corners of his mouth. He was laughing at me, I could tell, but I answered him anyway. "No. I always have nightmares the first night in a strange bed. But it was weird that it took that form, you know? I've never really given any thought to merfolk before. And I've been having the dreams pretty much every night since then."

"Like I said, it was probably just the power of suggestion." He shrugged. "Reading my book on top of everything probably isn't helping, either."

"Yeah, you're probably right." I thought for a minute. "So you believe Zach is dead?"

He nodded. "Yeah. I do. I think everyone pretty much does, just no one will say it. He was last seen heading for town on foot. I think someone must have stopped and taken him. No one in town saw him—unless of course they're all in on it and covering for each other, which is just about as likely as mermaids getting him and eating him alive."

I stood up. "I've taken up enough of your time."

"I don't mind at all. Stop by anytime. I'm always here." He laughed. "And I could stand a break from the monotony, to tell you the truth." I started to open the screen door when he stopped me. "Just be careful, all right, son? I don't want you to end up missing."

"Thanks." I put my foot on the top step, but stopped. "What did Zach want to know about? You know, when he came here?"

"He was curious about the Rossitters," Dr. Ricker replied. "Wanted to know if any of them were still around."

"Are there any around?"

He nodded. "Just one. Roger Rossitter. He lives on the beach on the other side of the Inn a ways." He shrugged. "You think he might have had something to do with him disappearing?"

I smiled. "I don't think anything, Dr. Ricker. Thank you for your time."

The screen door slammed behind me.

*Maybe it was just the power of suggestion,* I thought as I walked up his driveway. *But it's still pretty weird.*

A chill went down my spine. I felt like I was being watched.

I spun around and looked into the woods.

Everything was still.

*Maybe I'm just losing my mind,* I thought with a sigh as I started walking again.

## CHAPTER SEVEN

I gulped down water and took a quick shower to wash off the sweat before changing back into workout clothes. I was tired of eating sandwiches for dinner, and I needed to return Dr. Ricker's book to the library. I figured I might as well lift weights and do cardio at the gym since I had to go to the library anyway, and I could grab a late lunch at the Singing Mermaid.

The shower felt good. My skin felt tender. Too much sun, even with the sunscreen. Whenever I touched it, the place where my fingertip pressed turned white before going back to the reddish brown. I'd have to get a stronger sunscreen. I thought I was already tan enough that sunburn wouldn't be an issue. But the reflected sunlight off the water was apparently too intense.

I lathered up my body. *You don't believe in flesh-eating mermaids. There's no such thing. There aren't vampires or werewolves or witches or anything like that. You're scaring yourself. Like Dr. Ricker said, everything has a plausible explanation. This is all in your head. It's no wonder you're having nightmares. You've been obsessing about all this shit ever since you got here. If there were such a thing as killer merfolk out there in the water, someone would have discovered them already, it would have been all over the news, there's no way the Coast Guard or anyone would have allowed this to go on. You know that. You're making yourself crazy.*

I dried off and packed my gym bag. I sat on the bed and stared out the window for a moment.

I've never been afraid of the water.

I wasn't going to start being afraid now.

Zach Patterson's disappearance had nothing to do with the crazy legends.

I slipped the gym bag's strap over my shoulder and locked the door behind me. The hallway was hot as an oven, and I was sweating by the time I got to the bottom of the stairs to the third floor. The Inn was silent as always. Cecily was sitting at the desk in the office but I slipped by without saying anything.

The inside of my truck felt like a furnace. I turned the air conditioner up all the way, and after a moment the hot air blowing through the vents turned cold. I backed out of my spot and made a U-turn.

The parking lot at the gym was crowded, and I was lucky to even find a spot to park. I walked over to the library and slipped the book through the return slot. Margery was standing at the counter, sorting books. I waved but she didn't see me. I jogged back over to the gym. I don't like going to the gym when it's crowded. I liked to lift weights best when there was no one around. I never worried about needing a spotter because I never lifted weights too heavy for me to control. I usually only used dumbbells or machines, so getting trapped beneath a barbell wasn't going to happen. I wanted to get stronger, but I didn't want my muscles to get big and bulky. That would slow me down in the water.

I didn't want anything to ever slow me down in the water.

So I did low weights with a lot of repetitions per set. It made my muscles stronger and gave them more endurance. Most guys want big, bulky muscles. I always tried to use the weight room at Corinth High when there wouldn't be anyone in there. The football players and the wrestlers laughed at me when I worked out.

*"Why you lifting those girl weights?"*

*"Don't you want to look like a man?"*

*"Why don't you try lifting some real weight? Why are swimmers such pussies?"*

And they would laugh, always. They didn't care that I almost always won my races. They didn't care that I was a conference champion, or that I earned my way to the state meet every year since I was a freshman, or that I was the only successful athlete at Corinth High. Our football team stank and was lucky to win a few games per season. Most of the wrestlers had losing records.

That didn't get me any respect at Corinth High. Swimming wasn't a real sport to my idiot classmates. So I tried to avoid them as much as possible. At least in high school all the teasing about me being one of those white-trash Hackworths had finally died down. They still thought it, though. I could see it in their eyes and on their faces.

I just ignored them, the way I always had.

But on the inside I burned.

I pushed open the gym door. Air conditioning and loud techno music blasted over me. Weight plates clanked against other weight plates. The treadmills whirred as their belts moved and running feet touched down on them. Grunts and groans and an occasional strained explosive shout wove in and out of the notes of the music. I smelled sweat and musk and bleach. The door swung shut behind me. I hadn't really expected it to be this crowded. Apparently Latona had a lot of people who liked to exercise during their lunch hour.

But at least here, no one knew I was a white-trash Hackworth.

No one was going to judge me or make fun of me for the light weights I used.

I scanned my card just as Micah came out of the back room carrying a laundry basket filled with fluffy white towels. His arms and shoulders were flexed, veins popping out, even though the basket couldn't have been heavy enough to be a strain. His skin was darker than it had been the last time I'd seen him. A gold chain hung around his neck. His hair was now buzzed closer to his scalp.

He did a bit of a double take. "Haven't seen you in a while." He smiled as he set the basket down on the counter and started folding towels. I got a whiff of warmth and fabric softener. His eye had pretty much healed. There was still some slight yellow discoloration on the skin around the socket. The blood spot was gone. He was wearing a bright yellow tank top with *Bayside Fitness* stretched across his thickly muscled chest. The bright yellow made his tan look deeper and richer. "Was beginning to think you didn't like us!"

"Been busy with work," I replied. "You're just not here usually when I come in. I like to come in early. I don't like it when the gym's crowded."

"You must come in pretty damned early to get in and out before I get here." He gave me a broad wink. "You sure you don't want to get in the ring? You could make some serious money as a wrestler." He finished folding the towel in his hands and rested his elbows on the counter. The tank top fell open at the neck, giving me a good look at his smooth chest. "You need money, don't you? I'll be glad to help you out. I can think of any number of ways you could make money this summer."

"Thanks, that's very kind of you," I replied. "I'll think about it."

The showers were running in the locker room. There was a thick cloud of steam floating just below the ceiling. I found an open locker and locked up my bag. I sat on the bench for a moment, taking some deep breaths. One of the showers stopped running, and the glass door swung open. I got up quickly and headed back into the weight room. I put in my earbuds and pulled up a workout playlist on my smartphone. I walked over to the pec-deck machine and set the weights. I sat, took a deep breath, and started working.

When I was finished, I showered again and got dressed.

"Can I get a protein shake?" I asked Micah at the counter, setting my bag down. "Strawberry flavored?"

"Sure." He got me a premade shake out of the cooler. "That'll be five bucks." I dug out a five from my wallet and slid it across the counter. He rang it up on the computer and put the money in the drawer as I gulped it down. "Say, are you hungry?" he asked as he closed the register drawer.

I finished the shake and tossed the container into the trash. "Yeah, actually I am. I was thinking about heading over to the Singing Mermaid." I patted my stomach. "I love that place."

His face twisted. "After a workout you want to load up on breading and grease?" He shook his head.

"Cheat day. No guilt." I shrugged. "Besides, I'll burn it all off tonight when I go swimming in the bay."

"After working out here you're going to swim?"

I nodded. "It's my day off. I like to push myself. Don't you?"

He laughed. "Of course, but when you get to be my age, there's only so much pushing you can do—so live it up while you're young." He cocked an eyebrow upward. "That sounds kind of good, actually. I haven't had anything bad in a while. Mind if I join you? I'll even treat." He gave me a big grin, his blue eyes twinkling. "You can ride with me."

"Okay, great," I replied. I followed him out to the parking lot and got into his Jeep. I didn't comment on how odd it was that someone in such good shape and who owned a gym would drive the four blocks or so to the Singing Mermaid rather than walk. To each his own, I supposed, and it was pretty damned hot out.

The parking lot was crowded. Micah parked in the closest spot he could find to the door. He turned off the engine and smiled at me. "The Mermaid is a really happening spot on weekends—if you were older, of course. It's about the best time you'll find in Latona. Granted, that's a pretty low-set bar." He laughed and punched me in the arm lightly.

"Have you ever heard of a place called Dusty's?" I asked. "In Mobile, I think? Is that place fun?"

He looked a little startled at first. After a few moments his face relaxed and he winked at me. "You've heard of Dusty's? You sure are a fast worker." He put one of his big hands on my left leg and squeezed my inner thigh. "You know, I had a feeling about you the first time I saw you. Come on, let's get something to eat. We can talk more inside."

Garth Brooks's "Friends in Low Places" was blaring on the jukebox as I opened the door. I stepped aside and held it for Micah. He gave me another lewd smile and walked into the dim restaurant. The place was really crowded. We stood inside the door at first, scanning the room for a table. The *seat yourself* sign was still up. I saw Alana come out of the kitchen carrying a tray filled with steaming hot plates. She froze when she saw us and just stood there staring, her mouth open. Her eyes narrowed a bit when I smiled back at her.

Micah grabbed my arm. "There's a table in the back. Come on." I followed him through the tables crowded with food and arms. He sat facing the front of the building, and I took the chair across from him. "Man, this place is crowded today." He shook out a paper napkin and draped it across his lap. He put his big elbows down on the table, which shook a little. It wasn't totally level. "So what do you know about Dusty's?"

Alana appeared at our table before I could answer. She plastered a phony smile on her face as she handed the laminated menus to us. "Can I get you something to drink, gentlemen?"

"Hello, Alana." Micah gave her a big smile. She flinched slightly. It was barely noticeable. "I'll just have water." He rubbed his flat stomach. "The meal's going to bust my diet enough as it is."

"I'll have sweet tea with lots of lemons."

She nodded. "I'll get those for you and give you a chance to check the menu."

Micah watched her go. "Pretty girl," he commented as he turned his head back to look at me. "I've watched her grow up—she was always a pretty little girl. Good genes—her brothers are some good-looking boys too." His tongue ran along his lower lip. "They were jocks, all of them. She's the youngest."

"They own this place?"

He nodded. "The Pavones have done pretty well for themselves here. Her grandparents came over here from Italy after the war, opened this place up, and have been running this place ever since. Family business. The oldest boy, Dom, is probably going to take over when his father retires…not that Antonio shows any signs of ever wanting to stop working." He leaned back, putting both hands behind his head. His lat muscles fanned out, his biceps flexed, and I could see beads of sweat in the tawny hair under his arms. The skin beneath the hair was white and untanned. "So, you really should give my offer of training you in the ring some thought. You could make some serious cash, my friend."

"Wrestling's not really my thing." I shrugged. "I'm a swimmer." *And the wrestlers at my high school were total assholes.*

He put his elbows back on the table and leaned in. Veins popped out in his shoulder muscles. "You're trying to save money for college, aren't you? I'm giving you a chance to make some more— you can make in one night what you make in a week lifeguarding."

"That much?" I leaned back in my chair and folded my arms. "Just for wrestling?"

Before he could answer me, Alana put a red plastic glass in front of each of us. She handed me a straw. "Here're your drinks." Her tone was cold and unfriendly. "Have you decided on what to eat yet?"

Micah's eyes hardened as he looked at her, but his smile didn't falter. "I'll have the Mermaid platter."

"I'll have the same." I handed my menu back to her. She nodded and walked away.

"Now where were we?" His smile looked predatory, his big teeth gleaming in the dim light.

"You were telling me how much money I could make wrestling." I watched his face as he smiled again. "And I was listening. Wrestling's not my thing, but I am interested in making some extra money. Like you said, every bit will help this fall when I start school."

He winked at me, the big smile getting so wide it looked like he could swallow me whole. "You're a good-looking young man with a great body, Ricky. You could make a lot of money this summer." He snapped his fingers. "In fact, I know several ways you could make some money in no time flat."

"I'm always interested in making money." I took another drink of my tea, watching his eyes. "I appreciate it, Micah. Thanks."

He nodded and arched an eyebrow. "Good, glad to hear it." He drummed his fingers on the table. "I'm always looking for young men who want to make money." He leaned across the table. "And you're interested in Dusty's? Maybe we can take a trip up there this weekend. This Friday night work for you?"

"I'm not twenty-one," I replied. "I mean, if it's a bar I'm not old enough."

He smiled. "Don't worry about that, my friend—I can take care of that for you." His smile turned into a bit of a leer. "I got connections." He nodded his head slightly, licking his lower lip.

I bit my lower lip and smiled back at him. "That would be great. Yeah, let's do it. Dusty's, this Friday night."

He clapped his hands together and smiled as Alana placed our plates in front of us. She set his down so hard the food jumped. Some of the shrimp fell off onto his placemat. His smile never wavered as she snarled, "Let me know if there's anything else you want." She spun and flounced away.

"She doesn't like you much," I observed as I started salting my food.

"Not everyone is going to like you in this life, kid." He made a face and shrugged. "You can let it bother you and it'll eat you alive—or you can just say the hell with 'em and live your life." He speared a shrimp with his fork. "I've always said the hell with 'em, myself."

"Me too."

We didn't talk much while we were eating. Working out always makes me ravenous. The smell made my stomach growl. But I took my time, not wanting to burn the inside of my mouth with the hot, greasy food. Micah was like a buzz saw tearing through everything on his plate, moaning in ecstasy from time to time. He ate methodically, with big bites he washed down with big gulps of water.

Every once in a while Alana came by our table, refilled our glasses silently, and then moved away through the restaurant. Her step wasn't as bouncy as it had been the first day I'd seen her. Even her ponytail seemed to have lost its bounce. She never asked if everything was okay or if we wanted any dessert. When we were finished, she slapped the bill down on the table so hard the tea in my glass sloshed up. "Thanks guys," was all she said as she piled our plates and cutlery on a tray.

She *really* didn't like him.

He pushed his chair back. "I'll be right back—I'm going to the restroom." He walked away from us.

She glanced back over her shoulder and watched until he pushed his way through the men's room door. She leaned in close to me and lowered her voice. "Look, you seem like a nice guy, okay?" She glanced back again.

"Thanks, I think?"

"You need to stay away from Micah Gaylord," she whispered urgently. "He's bad news. If he's asking you to do something, say no. You don't want to get involved in anything with him, do you understand me?" She hesitated. "Seriously. I'm not making this up." Her tone was urgent, her eyes pleading. "You have to believe me, Ricky. Just stay away from him. I'm not crazy, trust me."

"I didn't think you were," I replied slowly. "And thanks for the warning, I guess."

"Look, I can't talk now." She scribbled something on her order pad, tore off the sheet, and passed it to me. "Please call me later. I get off work at nine tonight. Maybe we can meet on the beach or something, if you want to talk more. But whatever he wants you to do, say no." She spun on her toes and bounced away.

I took a drink from my iced tea. Now, *that* was interesting, I thought as I unfolded the order slip. *Please call me. Alana.*

Her phone number was written underneath.

She'd underlined the words twice.

I folded it and put it inside my wallet.

*Interesting.*

Micah came back to the table and slapped a ten down on the table as the tip and took the bill up to the cash register. He drove me back to the gym. "Sure you don't want to come in, get in the ring, give it a try?" His voice was wheedling.

*Hey, little boy, do you want some candy?*

I declined. "Thanks, though." I rubbed my stomach as I climbed out of the Jeep. "I need to get in the water and burn off some of those calories."

"All right." He smiled at me as he climbed out of the Jeep. He yawned and stretched, making sure I could see as his every muscle flexed. "Meet me here at the gym on Friday night at eight. And text me a picture of you, just the head and shoulders." He winked again as he turned the ignition key. "For the ID."

He watched as I got into my truck and waved as I drove off. The greasy food was sitting heavily in my stomach as I drove along Shore Road. I looked to see if Dane was around at Rocky's as I went past, but if he was there I didn't see him.

*He's connected to Dusty's too. What the hell is that place?*

I parked in the empty lot at the Inn and was soaked through with sweat by the time I got inside. Cecily was still in the office. I didn't see Joe anywhere as I went up to my room and showered yet again. I stretched out on the bed and took a long nap.

And had another nightmare.

Just like the other one, I was swimming in the bay. The sun was high in the sky and the water was like glass. Perfectly calm, perfectly still, not even the slightest flutter of waves on the surface as I worked my way through it doing the freestyle stroke. I was counting strokes, focusing on keeping a perfect rhythm as I moved through the water the way I always did.

And again, I saw the movement of something big, deep in the water beneath me. Just like the first time, I paused in the water as it came into view.

But this time the merman had Micah's face.

I sat up straight in the bed, almost banging my head on the slanted roof.

Nervously I got out of bed. I washed my face and brushed my teeth. It was getting late in the afternoon. I checked my e-mails, my Facebook News Feed. I was feeling antsy. My muscles were extremely tired, so a late-afternoon swim was out. My muscles needed rest. I lay down on the floor and went through a series of crunches—fifty, one hundred, two hundred, three hundred, stopping at four hundred as my lungs and stomach burned.

*What does he want from me? What exactly is Dusty's?*

The curiosity was eating me alive.

*Can't seem too eager. Don't want to push it, or scare him away.*

I got out the matchbook and looked at it.

Dane.

Dusty's.

Micah.

I picked up my phone and started to punch in Dane's number… but didn't hit send. *What would I say to him if I called him?* I didn't know what he wanted from me, either. I put my phone down.

I got up and started pacing. My stomach rumbled. The greasy food, the nap, and the crunches were not a good combination. I got a strawberry protein drink out of the refrigerator and gulped it down, hoping that might settle the dance going on in my stomach. I sat back on my bed, phone in my hand.

Alana wasn't off work until nine.

Should I call Dane?

I was so bored.

I stared at the ceiling.

Finally, unable to take it anymore, I slipped my feet into my sandals and headed out. The Inn was silent as I went down the steps. When we had guests, noise was going to seem weird. I didn't bother to check to see if Cecily was still in the office. I went out the back door and walked along the wooden bridge past the dunes. I walked down to the waterline. The tide was coming in again. The wind had picked up and it felt a lot cooler than it had been. There was a sailboat out there, skimming across the surface. I stood there, with my hands in my shorts pockets.

*It's so beautiful here.*

I started walking along the waterline, watching the gulls as they circled and swerved and dove at the water. So peaceful, so quiet, so alone. It felt almost like one of those movies where the hero was the last human left alive on the planet after some kind of holocaust or apocalypse.

"Ricky!"

I turned to see Cecily standing on the steps coming down from the bridge. I stopped walking. She didn't move. She didn't call again, didn't gesture for me to come to her. After a few minutes of staring at each other, I started walking through the sand. It scrunched under my feet the way it always did. Her face was expressionless as I approached her. She sat on the steps as I got closer. Her hair was pulled back in her standard ponytail. She had very little makeup on. She was wearing a Mermaid Inn T-shirt and a baggy pair of shorts.

"You called?" I asked, resting an arm on the signal post.

She looked at me without expression. "I heard you had lunch with Micah Gaylord today."

"News travels fast around here." I shrugged.

"Alana called me," she replied. "What were you doing having lunch with that man?"

"Why do you care? What's with the sudden interest in me, anyway?"

She blinked at me. "I don't know what you mean."

"You haven't exactly welcomed me with open arms," I replied. "You've made it pretty clear from the moment I arrived that you don't like me." I shrugged. "That's fine, you don't have to like me." *I'm used to not being liked.* "I'm just here to do a job, that's all. We don't need to be friends."

She stared at me for a few minutes without saying anything. The only sound was the waves and the squawking of the gulls. "Micah Gaylord is bad news, Ricky. You need to stay away from him." She looked back out over the water.

"Why would Alana call you and tell you that I had lunch with him?" I asked. "I don't understand."

"Dane Whitsitt is someone else you need to avoid." She scratched her head, still not looking at me. "There are some bad-news people in this town, Ricky. Maybe you should start thinking about going back home."

"You *sent* me to Dane Whitsitt, remember? Now you're telling me to stay away from him? Come on, what's this about? What kind of game are you playing?"

"No games, Ricky." She turned her head and looked me in the face. "You really think I'm stupid, don't you?"

"I don't think you're stupid."

She held my gaze. "You really don't know anything, do you?" She shook her head. "You came here completely blind, didn't you? You don't know a damned thing." She gave a bitter laugh. "Or you're a really good actor. I can't decide which. Which is it, Ricky? Who are you?"

"What are you talking about? You're not making sense."

"I know why you came here." She crossed her arms. "So you can stop pretending."

"I came here to work. Make some money for college. That's not a secret."

"So you're telling me none of this is an act?" She shook her head again and exhaled with an exaggerated sigh. "All this time I've been waiting for you to say something to me. I thought there was some reason you weren't saying anything, and this whole time it's been because you honest to God didn't know?" She barked out a harsh laugh. "He really didn't tell you anything?"

"Who? Who are you talking about?" I stared at her. "You're not making any sense, Cecily. Tell me what you mean."

"Zach."

The hairs on the back of my neck stood up. "Zach? Zach Patterson? How could he have told me anything? He's been missing for almost a year."

She blew out her breath in exasperation. "Don't you get it yet, Ricky? I know exactly who you are, and why you're here. I've known all along." She leaned closer to me. "Zach and I were friends, Ricky. He talked to me about things."

"So? What does that have to do with me?"

"So it means he told me things. He liked to talk, as you well know, because you were Zach's boyfriend." She crossed her arms and gave me a smug smile. "He told me all about you last summer. And my guess is you're here trying to figure out what happened to him. Are you going to stand there and still try to tell me you didn't know Zach?"

## CHAPTER EIGHT

I was twelve years old the first time I saw Zach Patterson.

It was at a swim camp on the University of Alabama campus. This was very first time going to a swim camp. I'd also never spent the night away from home somewhere that wasn't my grandparents' farm. I was nervous and scared to death. I wasn't worried about not making friends—life in Corinth had made me well prepared for that. I'd checked out a bunch of Agatha Christie mysteries to read when I wasn't in the pool. But not having Dad around was going to be weird.

It had been just the two of us for as long as I could remember. It was going to be weird not having dinner together every night and watching television together until we both went to bed. It was going to be weird not having coffee and breakfast with him in the morning before he went to work. It was only going to be five days, but they yawned in front of me like an endless summer. He'd told me any number of times if I wanted to come home, all I had to do was call him.

Afraid as I was, I wasn't about to do that. I'd grit it out if it killed me.

I wasn't going to disappoint my dad, not after he somehow managed to come up with the money for the camp. Not after my grandmother went to a fabric store and bought material to make me racing trunks so I wouldn't have to wear board shorts. I was nervous about wearing them in public for the first time. But I needed to get used to them. I'd have to wear them when I started swimming competitively in high school. I'd blushed furiously when I tried them on the first time.

It was like being naked.

Dad drove me to Tuscaloosa bright and early the day before camp started. He had work to do, so we had to go early. We loaded my battered old borrowed suitcases in the back of the truck. We didn't talk at all the entire forty-minute drive through the countryside. Dad put a Martina McBride CD into the stereo, and all the way to Tuscaloosa she wailed through the speakers. We got lost a couple of times trying to locate the check-in place for the camp. But finally we found the right building and parked. I checked in with a bored college girl and was assigned a dorm room. She gave me a map of the campus with the dorm where I'd be staying circled in red. It wasn't far, just a short walk from the aquatic center.

"You want me to drive you over there?" Dad asked. His eyes were red and watery.

I looked away, afraid I might start crying and make a fool out of myself in front of the college girls running the registration desk. "No"—I tried to keep my voice from quivering—"I think I can make it over there on my own, Dad."

"All right, then." His voice broke and he swallowed, patting me on the shoulder. "I'll go ahead and head home, then. Make me proud, son."

I watched him drive away. I wanted to jump back into the truck and go home. I was terrified. I didn't want to stay there by myself. I was a shy kid, even before I learned very young that a Hackworth was less than nothing in Corinth County. I didn't have any friends. I stayed away from other kids at school and ignored the horrible things they said about me. I refused to ever let them see how much the names hurt. I just ignored them, pretended they didn't exist, and focused on getting the best grades I could as they made fun of my clothes. They made fun of me for being poor. I hadn't even known we were poor until I started school. They made fun of me for not having a mother. They wrote nasty things about me on desks, blackboards, and even my locker. The teachers knew. How could they not, when some of the things were said in class? When they would shoot spitballs at me that stung my neck and the back of my head? I would just sit there, fighting back tears as I wiped the spitball off my neck or picked it out of my hair. Sometimes it was just a shove in the back, or my books would get knocked out of my hands.

I learned very young to stay away from them. I learned not to go out to the playground for recess. I found places to eat my lunch where no one else was around. Dad dropped me off at school every morning, and rather than take the bus and face more abuse, I just walked home every day.

I started swimming when I was ten. That was the summer when someone reported my dad to the county for leaving me home alone all day. The social workers came and they took me into a room alone and asked me a lot of questions, questions that even as a kid I found offensive and insulting. Did I get to eat regularly? Who did the laundry? Who cleaned the house? How often was I left home alone? Did my dad drink or do drugs? Did we go to church? It was endless, poking and prodding in that smug way I'd learned to hate, the way the counselors at school always talked to me. After they left, Dad told me he was going to get me into the swimming club at school. I already knew how to swim—Dad had taught me in the river behind my grandparents' farm. But this was different, and apparently my grandmother was going to pick me up after it was over and would stay with me until he got home.

"It's either that or they're going to take you away," Dad explained, his face sad. "Do you mind?"

I did but said no. I hated my grandmother. She chain-smoked and always stank like rotting teeth and sweat. She was mean too. She'd yell for no reason, or smack me whenever she felt like it. But if the only other option was spending the summer staying out in the country with her and my grandfather, I could handle this.

It was just something else to get through.

But swimming was an entirely different matter.

Sure, the same kids who treated me so bad were there—part of the reason I liked summer vacation was I didn't have to see them every day. But at swimming things were different, somehow.

Nobody bothered me there. Maybe it was because Coach Marren was so tough and strict. He wouldn't put up with any shenanigans, any playing around, any talking. He was tall and broad in the shoulders and chest. He'd been a competitive swimmer all through college and had even almost made the Olympics once. He didn't care about anything besides what you did in the water.

And I was at home in the water. I learned the other strokes—the breaststroke, the backstroke, the butterfly—quickly and easily. Any instruction Coach Marren gave me, I was able to incorporate. He taught me how to stretch with every stroke, to get as much distance as I could out of every one of them, how and when to breathe. Coach Marren pushed me and I responded. Other kids argued with him, cried in frustration, threatened to quit.

Not me. I just wanted to get back in the water.

I could outswim anyone in Corinth County. I could outrace some of the kids on the high school team, and the ones who could beat me barely did. Coach Marren thought I had potential. "Ricky, you could get a scholarship that would pay for college," he told me one day, pulling me aside after practice. "You could possibly even make the Olympics."

Going to the camp was his idea. I knew the money hadn't been easy for Dad to come up with. I didn't even know how much it was, but it had been pretty dear.

I wasn't going to let Dad down. Or Coach Marren.

I grabbed my bags and went into the dorm. My room was on the second floor: 245. I made my way down the hallway, crowded with jabbering teenagers of all shapes and sizes, kids who clearly knew each other from before camp. I felt even more isolated. No one paid any attention to me as I walked around the groups. *At least they're not making fun of my cheap clothes,* I thought as I found the door for room 245. It was standing open. I could hear a television on, an episode of *Law and Order.* I hesitated and rapped my knuckles on the open door before walking in. The room was pretty spartan. Two single beds made from processed wood, each with a nightstand on either side. The far wall had two enormous closets, with desks beside them with bookshelves going up the wall above them.

On one of the beds a tall blond kid was sprawled on his stomach. He was wearing just a white pair of briefs. He was reading a comic book.

"Hello." I managed to get the word out somehow.

The blond boy rolled over onto his back and smiled at me. "You must be my roomie. About time you got here." In one fluid motion he gracefully rolled off the bed and up onto his feet. He was my height, maybe a fraction of an inch taller. Braces glinted on his teeth. His white-blond hair was parted in the center but was messed up. He had a square jaw, and thick red lips. His bright blue eyes were symmetrically spaced on either side of a slightly turned-up nose. Thick blond eyelashes framed his eyes. His skin was golden. His body was muscled and lean. I could count the muscles in his flat stomach. His chest was broad and his hips narrow. "I'm Zach Patterson."

"Ricky Hackworth."

"You look like country," he said. The big infectious grin on his face, the deep dimples in his cheeks, the sparkle in his blue eyes, somehow managed to take the sting out of the words. "I'm from Montgomery. Where are you from?"

"Corinth."

"The Corinth Swim Club?" His brow wrinkled. "I've swum in meets with some of those kids. Your coach is a nice guy. How come I've never seen you at meets before?"

"I've never competed before." I put my bags down on the other bed. "I just joined the club a few months ago."

*After someone reported my dad as a bad parent because I came home to an empty house after school every day, and that I'd be alone by myself all summer. Bet you don't have those kinds of problems, do you? And those horrible people from Protective Services told him he had to either get me a babysitter or they might have to take me away from him. The Corinth Swim Club was the only after-school activity that made any sense and that we could afford. It didn't matter that I got home at six and sometimes Dad didn't get home until later. It didn't matter that I now had to spend the afternoons after coming home from the pool with my wicked witch of a grandmother. Because a mean old bitch who blew smoke in my face and backhanded me whenever she goddamned pleased was better than me being alone.*

"So you're new to swimming?" His smile didn't waver as he sat back down on the bed. He stretched out, putting his hands behind his head.

"I always knew how," I said as I opened one suitcase and started putting clothes into the drawers in the open closet. "I just learned how to do the other strokes this summer. Coach Marren thinks I have potential." My face was flaming. I never talked this much as a rule. "He thinks I can get a scholarship and go to college. No one in my family's been to college before. I'd be the first."

"Everybody in my family goes to college," Zach replied. "My dad's a lawyer and my mother's got an MBA."

I didn't know what that was but didn't ask. He was being so nice I didn't want to give him a reason to make fun of me.

"What will you do if you don't go to college?" he went on.

I finished neatly stacking my shirts and closed the drawer. I stored the now-empty suitcase under the bed. "I guess I would have to work with my dad or get a job at the rubber glove factory." The factory was just outside of town, on the road we took when we went out to my grandparents'. The melting rubber and plastic stank to high heaven, and I couldn't imagine what it would be like to work there and have to smell that all the time.

That's why Dad was so excited about the swimming. College was a chance for me to get out of Corinth County and actually have a better life than he'd ever dared to dream.

The Hackworths were white trash, always had been and always would be. Most Hackworths never finished high school. Nobody could forget that my dad's aunt had shot and killed her husband. Hackworths always had bad teeth and smelled dirty and drank too much and didn't go to church and weren't fit company for anyone. On my first day of school I found out exactly where I stood with the other kids—the teachers too. Kids made fun of me for my clothes, for not going to church, for not speaking properly. I got pushed and shoved and knocked down and punched. Nobody would sit by me at lunch. I didn't have any cousins to help—all the other Hackworths lived out in the country somewhere.

I was on my own.

So I stayed away from everyone else. I sat in the back of the room and didn't talk to anyone. I didn't have any friends and never expected to have any. Dad insisted that I had to get my high school diploma. I figured I could stick with it at least that long, and I just gritted my teeth.

But I dreamed about escape. When we watched television at night, I wondered what it would be like to live in New York or San Francisco or Los Angeles, where no one else knew what my last name meant. Every night when I went to bed, before I fell asleep, I wondered what it would be like to live someplace where I could start over.

Well, on the nights when I wasn't praying that I would die in my sleep.

And now, here I was at swim camp, where no one knew anything about me. It was a chance to be someone else, to start fresh with a bunch of kids who didn't care what my name was or about my clothes or any of that other stuff that made Corinth people look down their noses at us.

This Zach Patterson person didn't know that I lived in a crappy run-down house with a rusting tin roof. He didn't know that my dad cleaned pools and did yard work for assholes who treated him like crap, just so he could put food on the table. He didn't know my grandfather's sister-in-law was a murderess. He didn't know my grandfather had a still in the woods and sold moonshine in Mason jars for extra money. He didn't know anything other than I was his roommate for camp and was going out of his way to be nice. He wasn't like the kids of lawyers back in Corinth, snooty little shitheads who thought they were better than everyone else.

I wasn't even sure how to act around him. He was so nice, so friendly. And I wasn't used to that.

He was my first friend.

His father was a senior partner in a big corporate law firm in Montgomery. His mother had been a debutante, from a fine old family, and ran a big nonprofit. Zach was an only child and went to St. Thomas More Prep. I'd never heard of it before, but it was apparently *the* prep school for rich people to send their kids to in Alabama. He showed me their website on his laptop. It was beautiful, all red brick and white columns and manicured lawns. Their swimming pool was gorgeous. All the kids on the website were wearing the same outfit: the boys in khaki pants and blue blazers and white shirts, the girls in the same blazers with khaki skirts and white blouses. Apparently everyone who went there got into the college of their choice. It looked amazing.

It was so much nicer than Corinth County High School.

I couldn't even begin to wonder how much it cost to go to school there.

Zach was the nicest kid I'd ever met in my life. He wasn't anything like the kids I knew back home. He didn't make fun of my cheap Walmart clothes or treat me like I was inferior. He didn't make fun of me at all. He was funny and fun loving and smart and decent. He introduced me around to the other kids in our age group, and they were just as nice and friendly as he was.

At swim camp, I learned pretty fast that all that mattered was how you did in the water.

And I did great in the water. I loved everything about swimming. I loved the focus, the way my body felt as I was going through the water. I loved that the coaches at the camp were impressed with my natural ability. I loved that they taught me training routines to improve my speed and my endurance and make my strokes even smoother. I liked that adults didn't look down their noses at me. I liked that adults weren't talking to me with contempt on their faces and scorn dripping from their voices. I had friends for the first time in my life.

And for the first time in my life I was happy.

I also found out another difference of mine wasn't that big of a deal.

I'd always known I was different from the other kids, and not just being a Hackworth, either. I'd ignored their meanness and cruelties and viciousness for so long they'd moved on to other victims. Every once in a while someone might call me white trash, but those instances were growing fewer and further between, and I never responded, never gave them anything or any reason to keep with the taunting. And they tolerated me.

But once I got into junior high school I noticed that boys and girls started going steady, walked around holding hands, sneaking kisses when they thought no adult was looking. The sudden sprouting of body hair had brought awareness of urges, urges that I didn't understand. I already knew from movies and television shows that the natural order of things was boy plus girl, but I wasn't interested in girls. I found my eye wandering to boys. Watching them in gym class in their shorts and T-shirts, my growing awareness of hair under their arms, on their calves and forearms. Voices deepening and black hairs sprouting on chins. Pimples and body odor and musk and other things. I found myself watching the way their muscles moved. I'd always been more aware of men than women in movies and on the TV. I heard the other boys saying things like cocksucker and faggot and fairy and knew it was something dirty and nasty, something to be ashamed of.

Now I had a new secret, something new to add to the list of things about me to be ashamed of, something I had to keep hidden from everyone at school.

If they knew about this, my life wouldn't be worth living anymore.

My daydreams used to be about getting away from Corinth, going somewhere else where Hackworth didn't mean garbage to look down on, and starting over. Now I was daydreaming about other boys, about good-looking movie stars with muscular bodies and washboard stomachs and hard, round, firm buttocks. I tore Calvin Klein ads out of magazines and hid them under my bed, pulling them out after I could hear my dad snoring in his room and imagining myself kissing the models, putting my arms around them and pressing my body up against theirs.

And I was ashamed.

Ashamed of my thoughts, ashamed of myself, ashamed of my life.

If I ever had any doubts, my grandmother cleared them up for me one afternoon when we were waiting for Dad to get home so she could go on back out to the country.

I was reading a book—The Three Investigators series—that I'd checked out of the library. She was watching a talk show when some movie star come out on stage.

"Faggots." She snorted angrily, stabbing her cigarette out in the enormous ashtray precariously balanced on the arm of the chair she was sitting in. "They ought to be ashamed of themselves."

"Faggots?" I asked, looking up from my book.

"Men with men." She snorted, lighting another cigarette. "Men acting like women. Having sex with other men. It's a goddamned abomination, it is. The morals of this country have gone to hell." She sucked in smoke and coughed up some phlegm.

I didn't say anything. I just picked up my book and started reading again.

It was my dirty dark secret to keep.

Swimming was my escape. When I was in the water I didn't worry about it. I didn't think about other boys or Zac Efron or Taylor Lautner as I went through my strokes, knifing through the water and focusing on staying steady, on breathing properly, on making sure I was utilizing my body the way I needed to so I could do the best I could in the water. I didn't want anyone to notice me looking at them in their skimpy racing trunks, the way the Lycra clung to the hard butt cheeks, the way it left so little to the imagination in the front.

I fell in love with Zach that first day because he was kind to me and I wasn't used to being treated that way.

I was also overwhelmingly physically attracted to him as well. As that week went by, the attraction grew almost every day. There was nothing shy about Zach. He had no problem walking around in his tight briefs or even naked. When I mentioned it once—he kind of teased me about always pulling on a shirt or a pair of shorts to cover myself—he just laughed and said, "I've been swimming since I was a kid. I'm more at home in a Speedo than I am in a pair of jeans. I just don't really think about it."

I couldn't take my eyes off him. We were the same height. We had very similar bodies but he was in better shape than me since he'd been training as a swimmer for more years than me. There wasn't any extra weight anywhere on his long, lean body. Muscles rippled every time he moved. I dreamed about him every night too. My dreams were dirty—the dirtiest dreams I'd ever had about anyone. I longed for him to kiss me, to put his arms around me and pull me close against him, to run my hands all over his beautiful golden-tanned body and explore it, to taste his nipples and lick his skin. I wanted him so badly it ached.

And more than once I woke up in the middle of the night needing to change my underwear and wash myself off while he slept on in the other bed.

I didn't dare say anything. I didn't want to turn the only friend I'd ever known against me, to see the contempt and dislike and disgust in his blue eyes, to hear the revulsion in his voice as he realized who and what I really was.

The last night of swim camp we went back to our room after dinner. Zach shut the door and sat on his bed. "Are you going to any more swim camps this summer, Ricky?"

"No," I replied, turning away so he couldn't see the shame on my face. I lied. "I didn't know there were other camps. This is my first one, and my dad and I don't, you know, have a computer. But this was so much fun—I hope to be able to go to more next summer."

"If you're really serious about swimming, you really need to go to as many camps as you can," he went on. "You just can't beat the training and experience you get…plus you get to see the people you're going to be competing against during the season." He sighed. "I really enjoyed this week with you, Ricky. I'm going to miss you."

"I doubt that," I replied, still not able to look at him. After all, he was going back to a life of country clubs and money and a prep school and all of his friends. I was going to miss him far more than he was going to miss me. I was going back to Corinth and no friends, to being watched every time I went into a store to make sure I didn't shoplift something because I was a no-account white-trash Hackworth.

"You don't even have a cell phone or a computer," he went on. "How am I supposed to stay in touch with you?"

"We have a landline." I got up and turned my back to him, starting to put my dirty clothes into my duffel bag. "You can call me there."

I felt his hands on my shoulders. He was standing right behind me, so close I could feel the heat from his skin on my back. His hands started massaging my shoulders, finding the knots and digging into them.

I couldn't hold back the tears.

"Shhh, don't cry," he whispered into my ear, gently pressuring me to turn around so we were facing each other. His face was very close to mine. I could feel his breath on my skin.

"This has been the best week of my life," I managed to get out around the sobs racking my body. "I don't want to go back home."

He put his arms around me and kissed my cheek. "It'll be okay."

I sat on the bed. "No, it won't," I said, and in spite of myself it all came tumbling out of me. How horrible school was, what it was like to grow up in Corinth as a Hackworth, how I had no friends. I'd never talked to anyone about it. He just kept kissing my cheek, holding me tightly as the words poured out of me, interrupted by choking sobs, and then we were lying on the bed next to each other, our arms around each other, and we were kissing.

And he kept his word. He called me without fail every few days to check in on me, make sure I was practicing and doing everything I needed to. He told me what camps he was going to, and I looked up the costs and discussed them with Dad and Coach Marren. I felt bad because I could tell it was going to be difficult for Dad to come up with the money, but he wanted to, because he wanted a better life for me and he saw this as my ticket out of the rubber glove factory. Coach Marren looked for ways to help, finding out if there were scholarships for kids from disadvantaged backgrounds like mine.

I looked forward to the calls from Zach. He told me everything. He told me about his friends and his own training, his parents, and things that went on at St. Thomas More Prep. The calls were the highlight of my week.

I could tell that Dad was happy I finally had a friend.

I worked very hard over the next school year so I could help out with the cost of the camps the next summer, so I could room with Zach, be with him. I got a cheap pay-as-you-go phone. I missed him so much when we were apart, my heart ached for him…and then I'd see him at every summer swim camp, I'd see him at swim meets, and we had to pretend not to be in love.

But we were in love. The time apart never seemed to matter.

As we got older we were able to see each other more often. Once Zach had his driver's license he could come up and visit. Sometimes Dad would let me take the truck down to Montgomery to visit him. The Pattersons lived in a manner I couldn't relate to. His parents were nice to me but distant. I got the sense they were too busy to really spend much time with Zach, either.

And even though he'd also gotten a scholarship to Alabama, and we'd already decided when I got there we'd share a room, he wanted to spend the summer after his senior year working at Mermaid Inn and saving his own money. Even though we were roughly the same age, he was a year ahead of me in school. He'd done two years in one in grade school, and he turned eighteen right before he graduated—I wouldn't be eighteen for another few months.

"My parents will never accept me being gay," he said to me on the phone. "If they ever find out, they'll cut me off. So I want to make sure I have a cushion."

I didn't understand. His parents were smart, educated. My father didn't care when I told him the truth about me and Zach, the truth about me. How could they cut off their only son when my uneducated father accepted me as I was?

So, he went to Mermaid Inn to work for the summer. He still called and e-mailed and texted me regularly, but I got the sense he was holding something back from me. I wasn't sure what was going on and it made me nervous.

And then he disappeared without a trace.

The local police didn't seem to care, never made any progress.

He was gone and no one cared besides his parents.

And me.

I had to find out what happened to him.

## CHAPTER NINE

We stared at each other in silence, Cecily sitting on the steps and me leaning against the railing.

Gulls screamed overhead and the waves continued to lap at the shoreline behind us. I wasn't sure what to say to her, or what I should believe. Could Zach have told her about us? It was possible, after all. Zach was friendly and talkative. It was one of the reasons I loved him so much. I envied him that ability. And he was so good-looking, with his golden-tanned skin and the white-blond hair and the deep blue eyes. He used to joke with me about the girls at school who had crushes on him, passing him notes in class or slipping them through the vent into his locker. Some of them came to his swim meets and took pictures of him emerging from the pool, water dripping off him and his wet trunks gripping every inch of him. I felt sorry for them. They didn't have a chance with him, and it seemed mean to me for him to laugh at them. It wasn't out of the question Cecily would have had a crush on him—it would have been weird if she hadn't. It could also explain why she'd been so distant and almost rude to me from the moment I arrived.

"He never mentioned you to me," I said slowly. I sat on the bottom step and rested my hands on my knees. "He seemed to change once he got here. He didn't seem himself, you know what I mean?"

"I don't," she replied. "I only knew him here. I don't know what he was like before." She shrugged. "He was so friendly and funny…I really had a crush on him, you know, from the moment he arrived. So good-looking, and that body!" She sighed. "But you know all that, don't you?"

"We used to talk all the time," I said, looking out to sea. "But once he got here, I mean—it's hard to explain. He still called the way he always did, texted and e-mailed, but I got the feeling he was holding something back from me. To be honest, I thought maybe he'd found someone else. I was so worried." I rubbed my eyes. "And then…silence. Nothing. He was just gone." I exhaled. "Maybe I'm crazy, but I don't think he would have just disappeared without telling me." I rested my head against the railing. "I knew from the beginning that he was dead. I knew when he didn't call me that Sunday something was wrong." I swallowed. "Maybe I just don't want to believe he would run off and not tell me. Maybe I'd rather believe that he's dead. You were here. You talked to him. Did he say anything to you?"

"He didn't tell me everything, either." Cecily slid down the steps until she was sitting beside me and put her hand on my forearm. "There was something going on with him. And his parents—they didn't want to listen to me. No one wanted to listen."

"Do you know why he came to work here? That never made sense to me."

"He didn't tell you about the big fight he had with his parents?" When I didn't answer, she went on. "I guess he didn't. A few months before the end of the semester, he decided to tell his parents the truth about who he was." She squeezed my knee. "He was tired of lying to them, and he wanted them to know about you, what was really going on between the two of you."

"He never told me about that."

"Yeah, well, it didn't go well." She sighed. "They told him if that was what he wanted, they weren't paying for school or anything for him anymore. So he got the job here, to help pay for school that fall. He had a scholarship but he needed other money too. He thought they'd change their minds eventually…I guess that's why he didn't tell you."

"He didn't want me to feel bad." I closed my eyes and clenched my fists. *You could have told me, Zach, I wouldn't have blamed myself.* "I felt so bad for him," she went on. "He was really hurting. I kept telling him he should talk to you about what was going on with his parents."

"I knew something was wrong." I put my own hand on top of hers. "Zach was always an open book. He told me *everything.* If anything, sometimes I thought he was too open with his feelings and what was going on in his life. He would pretty much talk to anyone about anything." I looked out to sea. "I knew something had changed when he told me he was taking the job here and not going to any swim camps over the summer for extra training. He'd been talking about how hard he wanted to train before he got to college." I smiled at the memory. "He wanted to show up and blow everyone out of the water. And then he changed his mind, came down here. It wasn't like him. I *knew* it was something else." I slammed my fists down on my knees. "I never really believed what his parents said about him working here." His parents told reporters Zach had wanted to earn his own money and stand on his own feet.

*We were so proud of him,* his mother's voice had choked in the televised interview. *Wanting to be a man and not be dependent on us anymore.*

That had never sat right with me.

Zach was never really a dick about coming from a family with money like so many other spoiled rich kids. He never flaunted it or rubbed my face in it. He did hate that I was poor. He hated that it was such a struggle for my father and me to pay for my swim camps. But he never made me feel bad about it. He never made me feel like the inexpensive gifts I got for him, little things like UA key fobs, weren't appreciated, and he never made me feel bad by getting me anything ridiculously expensive. His gifts were always special, the kind where I could tell he'd put some serious thought into the selection and listened when I talked.

That meant the world to me, made the presents all the more special.

He was kind, he was thoughtful, and he was a great guy.

He was not the kind of guy who would just disappear by choice.

There had never been any doubt in my mind he was dead.

"We hit it off from almost the moment he arrived," Cecily said. "He was so nice—I've never met a boy so good-looking and *nice* before. And funny! My God, he was funny. He could always make me laugh. I could tell there was something wrong, though… something that weighed on him, you know? He never talked about his parents—never, other than relief at being away from them for the summer—until he finally opened up to me about them cutting him off. I still can't believe parents could actually do that to their only child." She shook her head. "But after he…he disappeared, they acted like—well, you know. Their relationship was close, they were a perfect family, all of that *Leave It to Beaver* shit. It drove me crazy listening to them lie to the cops and the reporters." She made a face. "I guess they didn't want to let the whole world know what shitty parents they actually were."

"I don't know," I replied. I stood and paced around at the foot of the stairs. "They *were* close, though. Not as close as me and my dad, but close. They adored him. They might not have had a lot of time for him, but I mean, it was always pretty obvious to me." I scratched my head. "If someone would have told me they'd react that way to him being gay, I wouldn't have believed it. Zach was nervous about it, but I don't even think he had any idea how bad it would be." I took a deep breath and let it out again. "None of the news reports—and believe me, I watched every one of them and read all the stories to the point where I practically know them by heart—mentioned his sexuality. Never once did his parents say he was gay. They certainly didn't want anyone else to know."

"Other than that one time, he never mentioned them. If I brought them up, he changed the subject. It must have been really bad, the way it went down," Cecily admitted. She laughed. "Besides swimming and college, the only part of his life at home he would talk about was you." She rolled her eyes and squeezed my forearm. "He loved you so much…it made me jealous. Not of you, I mean. Jealous that he was so in love and was loved back so much. Okay, I was a little jealous. But you know, he could have been a dick about my crush on him, but he wasn't. He was such a great guy. He was so understanding."

"Yeah." I nodded. My head was whirling. Why didn't he tell me any of this? Why didn't he say anything to me about Cecily?

As the shock began to wear off, I wondered if I could actually trust her.

*But she knew about me. How could she have known about me and Zach if he hadn't told her?*

*His phone and his laptop never turned up.*

I didn't like being so suspicious, but at the same time I didn't want to meet the same fate as Zach.

*Why didn't he tell me what was going on?* I wanted to scream it out in frustration.

The last year had been so awful. I would never forget that morning when Mrs. Patterson had called me, her voice quivering, asking me if I'd heard from Zach or knew where he might be. My heart had sunk and my stomach twisted into knots as she told me, haltingly, about how he had walked out of Mermaid Inn two nights earlier and was never seen again.

"So, what exactly happened the night he disappeared?" I finally said. I'd wanted to ask her this ever since I arrived but wasn't quite sure how to go about it. It wasn't something you could just casually drop into conversation with someone who clearly didn't like you.

She took a few moments before saying anything. "He distanced himself from me too." She shook her head. "I wondered if I'd done something to piss him off, or what. I knew it had something to do with Micah and Dane." Her voice shook. "Dane showed up here one day, just hanging out at the beach—"

*I don't like the water,* I heard him saying to me again.

"—and Micah too. I mean, we can't stop people from using it, you know? We don't let people park in our lot and they can't go through the Inn to get to it, but they can park down the road and walk down." She shivered. "Dane's a creep. Handsome, but a creep. And then Micah started showing up here too, out of the blue. That was in early July. And that's about the same time when Zach didn't want to hang out as much with me and Alana—"

"Alana?"

She nodded. "Yeah, she's my best friend. The three of us would do stuff together. I mean, go to movies or get something to eat together, you know? Just friend stuff. She was the one who told me that she'd seen Zach hanging out with them, and she was worried. One of her brothers had gotten involved with them once—"

I heard Micah's voice saying *Yeah, her brothers are good-looking guys. Athletes, with great bodies.*

"—her brother Gianni, he wanted to be a professional wrestler like Micah used to be. He would never tell her why he stopped training with him, but it must have been pretty bad."

"He asked me to train with him, said I could make a lot of money wrestling."

"I don't think it's just wrestling." She exhaled. "I don't know what else it is, but it's not just wrestling. That's all Gianni would tell her. He also moved away right after, if that tells you anything. He wanted to get away from Latona. And he hasn't come back to visit even once."

I got up and walked away from her, back down to the waterline. This whole thing was a mess.

I remembered the e-mail he'd sent me about getting the job.

*Ricky,*

*I know this is going to seem strange and abrupt but I've taken a summer job lifeguarding at a place called Mermaid Inn. It's south of Mobile in a little seaside town called Latona. It just seems like the right thing to do. I need to do a lot of thinking about things before school starts this fall, and being away from my parents and even from swimming for the summer just makes the most sense to me. I wish I could explain it to you in a way that makes sense...but right now I can't. This just seems right to me. It doesn't change the way I feel about you—I still love you very much and long for the day when we can live together in Tuscaloosa—but this is important to me and you're just going to have to trust me. Do you love me enough to trust me? I hope so.*

*All my heart,*
*Zach*

What could I do but trust him? Even as questions raced through my mind, as I worried and wondered what was going on with him, I didn't press or push him. The e-mail was so damned cryptic, and the next time when we talked on the phone, he asked me to trust him again.

I accepted it. What other choice did I have? When he was ready to tell me, he would. All I could do was be supportive.

Had I known I would never see him again...things would have been different.

Since his disappearance I'd done nothing but second-guess myself. Why hadn't I demanded he tell me what was going on? I felt responsible. And the worst part was not being able to come down to Latona to look around, to find out what happened to him. People don't just disappear into thin air. Someone knew something.

And wasn't talking.

I'd spent my entire senior year trying to put it out of my mind. I focused on my training and getting good grades. I swam every morning. I went to class. I swam every afternoon. I won all my events at the conference meet. I finished in the top three in all of my events at the state championship meet.

But every night, after I finished my homework, I'd just lie in my bed staring at the ceiling, wondering what had happened to Zach.

So I'd decided to apply for the job at Mermaid Inn for the summer after my graduation. I talked to my dad about it—he didn't think it was a great idea, but he understood and supported my decision. He just warned me to always be careful, and to check in with him every night. I knew, though, if I disappeared...it wouldn't be the same as when Zach did. Two lifeguards in two consecutive summers disappearing?

Surely whoever had killed Zach wouldn't dare.

And if anything happened to me, my dad would call the Pattersons.

But the Hamptons hired someone else, and my plans were ruined. And then that someone changed his mind.

I walked back to the stairs and sat down.

"If I'd known you'd applied back in April, I would have made sure Uncle Joe hired you instead of that other kid," Cecily said. "Zach talked about you so much—I wanted to meet you. I knew there was a reason you were coming down here, but I wasn't sure why. I kind of thought maybe you wanted to come down here for closure or something. When Uncle Joe told me he'd hired you, I almost fell out of my chair. But I didn't know how much you knew, what you didn't know, why you were coming." She shrugged. "It was possible, after all, that you were just doing this as a way to say good-bye. And you made it pretty damned clear, from the minute you arrived, Zach had said nothing to you about me…which kind of hurt."

"All he ever said about this place was how pretty it was," I said. "The job was easy, it was really pretty here, and he had a lot of time to think." I exhaled. "The only person he ever mentioned was Dane Whitsitt. He also mentioned Bayside Fitness and the Singing Mermaid. But he never mentioned you or your uncle."

"Dane Whitsitt." Cecily ran a hand through her hair. "I warned him about Dane. Alana did too, I know." She cracked a smile. "Alana is how I know you had lunch with Micah Gaylord. She was worried you wouldn't call her tonight, so she called me."

"Were you the one who put the matchbook from Dusty's in my room?"

She had the decency to blush. "That was Zach's, yes. He dropped it in the lobby the morning before he…before he disappeared. I kept it."

"Why didn't you give it to the police?"

"The police." She snorted. "They didn't try too hard, you know? I told them everything I knew. Everything. So did Alana, and it didn't do a damned bit of good. They either didn't believe anything we said or didn't care." She sighed. "I tried to talk to the Pattersons too, when they came down here—but who listens to a teenager? Adults only listen to other adults. And the cops were doing a pretty damned good job of covering this whole thing up, sweeping it under the rug." She got up and walked down to the water's edge. I followed her.

"So you think the cops are protecting someone?" A chill went down my spine. *Maybe this is too big for me. Maybe I should pack my stuff and get out of here.*

But that wasn't possible. I'd committed to this and I couldn't back out of it now.

"Zach isn't the first guy to disappear around here." She shrugged. "I don't know, Ricky. But if that's the case, if the police are covering up for someone, it has to be someone pretty powerful around here."

"What about this Dusty's place?" I asked. "Micah is taking me there this weekend. He's getting me a fake ID so I can get in. Do you know anything about it?"

"I don't think you should go." She grabbed my arm, her fingernails digging into my skin.

"Ouch," I said, pulling my arm away. "Not with the nails, okay?"

"Sorry." She sighed and started walking. I walked alongside her. "I know Zach went there, and it was after he went there the first time he changed. He became more secretive and pulled away from me and Alana, both. We've talked about it I don't know how many times. We even drove up there once, to see what we could find out. We didn't find anything. Nobody will talk about Dusty's." She turned red. "I even used the passkey and searched his room while he was out here working one afternoon."

"You haven't done that to me?" I was only half joking.

"No. I suppose I deserve that. But I was worried, Ricky. His behavior changed so much. Instead of hanging out here or asking me to do something with him...after he went to Dusty's that first time, every night when he got off work he'd go back to his room, hang out there for a while, and then take off, going into town. He made it very clear to me I wasn't welcome to go with him too. And he wouldn't come back until really late at night. Sometimes it was the next morning. He'd come in, change into his lifeguard gear, and come back out here. I was terribly worried. I tried to talk to him but he wouldn't listen to anything I had to say. And then...he disappeared. Walked into town one night and never came back."

She sighed. "I found a wad of cash in his room, Ricky. I counted it. It was at least five thousand dollars, all rolled up and rubber-banded together. Now, what could he have been doing to get that kind of money? In cash? I mean, think about it. What does someone do to make that kind of cash?"

"You think he was dealing drugs?" I stared at her. "I can't believe that. Zach hated drugs. He hated it when other swimmers would smoke pot around us." *This need to make as much money as possible—because his parents cut him off. No wonder they were so upset. If they hadn't been such dicks to him when he came out, he would have spent the summer in Montgomery and gone to swim camps like he did every summer. He would still be alive. They were just as responsible as whoever it was who'd killed him.* "Did he ever say anything to you about training to be a wrestler with Micah?"

Her eyes widened. "No, I don't think he was dealing drugs." She whistled. "All I've been able to find out about Dusty's is it's a private men's club. Whatever that means."

"I guess I'll find out this Saturday," I replied. "Micah said I could make a lot of money there..." I shook my head. Men's clubs usually were strip joints, weren't they? But how could a guy make so much...

He couldn't have been *that* desperate for money.

But if he had been whoring himself out, that could explain why he'd become so distant. Why he didn't want me to know what he was doing. Why he didn't want the girls to know, either.

Oh my God. I felt sick to my stomach.

She slapped at a dragonfly buzzing around her head. "It doesn't look like much, you know, just a small place with a parking lot and not really much of a sign, even. It was closed—it doesn't open until eight." She shrugged. "I've done some snooping around online, talked to some kids in Mobile to see if they knew anything about the place. It's a gay bar, but it's members only, not open to the general public. But I only found one kid in Mobile who knew anything about it—he said his uncle was a member, and that's how he knew."

"A members-only gay club?"

She nodded. "That's what he said."

"Then Micah must be a member, otherwise how could he get me in?" I thought about this for a moment. "And obviously, Zach got in, right?"

"The matchbook doesn't prove that," she pointed out. "All that proves is that Dane wrote his phone number on it and gave it to him."

"It means Dane knows about it." I could hear him saying to me, *If you get bored give me a call.* I crossed my arms. "Maybe I need to give Dane a call."

"Wait till you talk to Alana," she replied. "She'll let you know all you need to know about him—and Micah."

"Why can't you just tell me?" We started walking back in the direction of the Inn. "Why all this mystery?"

"It's her story to tell." She shook her head. "I'll call her and tell her to just come over here after she gets off work." She glanced at her watch. "I need to run some errands in town. Promise me you won't do anything until you've talked to Alana."

We started up the wooden stairs. "Okay, I won't. Thanks."

She laughed. "I got tired of waiting for you to say something to me. It never occurred to me you didn't know—that Zach hadn't told you we were friends."

I smiled back at her. *But I only have your word for it.*

As I climbed the stairs back to my room, my mind was whirling. No one had ever found Zach's phone. It made sense he would have taken his phone with him, so it wasn't a mystery what happened to it. Whatever happened to him, he had his phone with him. But that didn't explain what happened to his computer. He wouldn't have taken his computer with him if he were going to a private club in Mobile. Both Joe and Cecily had told the police he hadn't been carrying a bag or anything with him when he'd left that night.

So whoever had his computer would have access to his entire life. His e-mails to and from me, his pictures, everything.

But if Cecily was somehow involved, it didn't make sense for her to make sure I got the job here.

Unless they wanted to find out what I knew, if they were worried I might know something that was dangerous to them.

I was going to have to be very, very careful. She'd already admitted she'd used the passkey and searched the room when it had been Zach's.

I was glad my laptop was password protected.

I didn't like what she'd implied about Zach's parents. I'd met them a number of times—stayed at their house in the guest room. Zach would always sneak in and join me after they'd gone to bed. I never got the sense they were homophobic, but Zach would never tell them the truth. *I know them better than you do,* he always said whenever I'd bring it up, and that would be that.

But what she'd said made sense. If they'd cut him off, that would explain why he took the job. It explained why he'd become a little distant with me—he didn't want me to blame myself for the rift with his parents.

But if they'd cut him off somehow, surely they wouldn't have let him keep the car and bring it down here, would they?

*What were you up to, Zach? What did you find out? What the hell was going on with you? Why didn't you tell me any of this?*

I read for a while and took a nap.

I dreamed again about the bay. I was swimming, desperately trying to get away from the mermen and their teeth, their claws. I couldn't get away, no matter how hard I swam, no matter what I did they surrounded me, their claws and their teeth tearing at my skin, their underwater calls and laughter ringing in my ears as I screamed and swallowed mouthful after mouthful of water, as my lungs filled and I couldn't breathe and their faces, their mad faces, were in mine, and I was sinking into oblivion…

I sat up in bed gasping for air. Someone was knocking on my door. The clock on my nightstand said it was about nine thirty. I got up, stretching and yawning, as the terror from the nightmare faded away. "Coming," I called when the knock came again. I quickly washed my face and brushed my teeth.

When I opened the door, both Alana and Cecily were standing in the hallway. Alana was still in her work clothes and smelled of grease and sweat. I invited them in, got a bottle of water for each of us. They sat down at my table. I opened my water and sat on the edge of my bed.

"Cecily tells me you're going up to Mobile with Micah on Friday night," Alana said, reaching behind her and pulling the rubber band out of her ponytail. She shook her head until her bluish-black hair settled onto her shoulders.

"You have a story to tell me about Micah and Dusty's?" I replied. "Something to do with Dane?"

"My brother Gianni," she said solemnly. "He had a big fight with my mom and dad, threatened to move out." She shrugged. "Micah took him there. I don't know what happened to him there—he would never say—but after that one time he calmed down and made peace with our parents. He won't talk about it, to this day, just says that there are some places that are best to be avoided. Dane, he used to come to the restaurant. He's nice looking, he would flirt. One night I thought Gianni was going to explode when he saw Dane flirting with me. He threw Dane out, told him never to come back again, told me to stay away from guys like him. He was bad news, Gianni said. And then Gianni moved away. But he told me if he ever found out I was messing with Dane, he would kill us both." She looked worried. "When Cecily told me Zach was going there, you can imagine what I thought. I tried to warn him, but he wouldn't listen to me, told me he knew what he was doing and he could take care of himself. A week later he was gone. Poof. Like he never existed."

"Why didn't you have your brother talk to the police?"

"Gianni doesn't live around here anymore. He joined the military. He's stationed in San Diego. He wouldn't have talked to the police, anyway." Her eyes flashed. "The police are in someone's pocket, you know. They don't care about Zach. Cecily and I tried to tell them, tried to get them to listen to us, but they couldn't be bothered." She shook her head. "You cannot go there, do you understand?"

"I have to find out what happened to Zach," I replied, "or at least try. And if it means going to this place, then I have to."

They exchanged looks. "I don't think it's safe for you to go there," Alana said.

"Please don't do this, Ricky," Cecily pleaded.

"You said you think the police are in someone's pocket," I said to Alana. "Cecily thinks so too. Who do you think it is?"

Alana shrugged. "The only person around here with that kind of money or pull is Roger Rossitter."

*Roger Rossitter. Dr. Ricker brought him up too.*

"We're going to come up there on Friday night," Cecily said, and Alana nodded, "just to keep an eye out for you. We can't go inside, obviously, but at the very least we can go to the police if something happens to you."

I wasn't sure I could trust either of them, but I agreed.

## CHAPTER TEN

The rest of the week flew by much faster than I expected. I spent Wednesday in much the same way as I had on Tuesday. I got up before the sun rose and had a protein shake and some coffee before going for my two-hour swim. The sun came up as I swam, heating my skin and lighting up the dark water. Lap after lap after lap, stroke after stroke, breath after breath, until my muscles burned and my lungs were aflame, until I emerged from the sea, depleted and exhausted and dripping. Back inside to my little apartment for an enormous breakfast. I made scrambled eggs with fried bacon and sausage, toast and orange juice. I wolfed it all down before going back to bed for another two-hour nap. That nap was dreamless—no trace of the recurring nightmare of the terror in the bay, of the mermen chasing me through the water and feasting on me.

I decided to skip the gym for a few days, instead doing two hundred push-ups and three hundred crunches in my room when I got up. I showered and examined my body for stubble. I was clearly due for another full-body shave but decided to put it off until Friday. I had a hunch it would be better to be smooth for Dusty's. I got dressed and drove into town. I parked my truck at the library lot and walked back down to the bay highway. I walked deeper into Latona, window-shopping and looking around.

Latona wasn't really that much different from Corinth in that way all small towns are the same. There was a languid pace and no one seemed to be in much of a hurry. There was a Walgreens and a Winn-Dixie, furniture stores and bait shops, convenience stores and clothing stores, a photography studio and gas stations. There were several junk stores that called themselves antique shops, a magazine stand, and fast-food places galore. The breeze from the bay was cool and strong. All along the shoreline there was a lot of activity on docks and at the marina. There was a strong fishy smell from the bay and, everywhere, Spanish moss hanging from huge live oaks. It was a cozy little town where everyone seemed to know everyone else, where young women pushing baby strollers stopped and talked to other young women with baby strollers.

I eventually reached the end of the business strip and turned around to walk back. I stopped at a Shop & Go to buy a big bottle of water. I was sweating when I got back to the truck. I went into the library to check out some books and Margery helped me print out some research about local disappearances before I headed to the Piggly Wiggly to buy some more food.

As I was taking my groceries out of the dumbwaiter I heard raised voices coming from the Hamptons' apartment. Cecily and Joe were either having an argument or a rather heated discussion. Their voices were muffled by the walls. I couldn't help but listen as I went back and forth from the dumbwaiter to my room lugging my groceries. I couldn't hear anything clearly but was able to make out a word here and there—*money* and *bank* and *mortgage*. As I put my groceries away, I couldn't help but wonder if my paychecks were going to clear.

I went back to my room, and as I lay down on my bed to read printouts of articles about other disappearances in the area, I couldn't help but think how expensive the Inn must be to operate. As Margery had mentioned casually as she'd helped me print out stories from the Latona paper, you've got to run the air around here 24/7 during the summer to keep the damp out, to keep out mold and mildew.

I took notes as I read, charting the facts in a neat Excel spreadsheet. It was very strange. There was never more than one disappearance per year, and some years there weren't any, but not even the newspaper reporters appeared to connect any of these dots.

Let alone the Latona police department.

It did kind of look like someone was being paid off to look the other way.

And why didn't the private eye the Pattersons hired turn up any of this stuff? I wasn't even a trained investigator. I e-mailed my notes to my dad just in case something happened to me and my computer disappeared like Zach's had.

I spent the rest of the day trying to find anything online about Roger Rossitter, but other than the occasional mention on the Latona newspaper's website, there wasn't anything. He clearly kept a low profile—or maybe he paid people to keep his online record clean. I'd read somewhere you could do that if you had enough money.

If you had enough money anything was possible.

That just made me all the more curious about him. There was only one photograph of him on the paper's website. He was wearing a suit, and it wasn't exactly a clear photo of him. It was also several years old. He was cutting the ribbon for the grand opening of the library, which apparently he'd pretty much funded. He seemed like a good-looking man, in his early forties, maybe.

There was no address listed for him online.

Curiouser and curiouser.

Thursday was a busy day at the Inn—finally—with families checking in and their teenagers coming down to the beach. Girls in skimpy bathing suits I was surprised their fathers let them wear in public, slathering their bodies with coconut-scented oils and lotions before lying down on enormous beach towels in supplication to the sun god. Their brothers tossed footballs and yelled and shouted as they splashed in the water and did typical boy things. I kept an eye on them all, making sure the little kids were in the shallow water and the bigger ones with their rafts and tomfoolery weren't drifting too far from shore. It seemed like all day long I could hear cars pulling into the parking lot, doors being slammed, and then footsteps coming down the bridge past the dunes to the beach. Other people wandered down from the direction of town, and I remembered Cecily saying townies would park along the highway and walk down. The beach reeked of sweat and coconut and lanolin intermingled with the fishy scent of the bay itself. The sky was cloudless and the sun beat down relentless from the azure sky.

All of this had to be good business for the Inn. I wondered if that meant Cecily and Joe might relax a little about money.

I didn't know what the nightly rates were, but if the number of people who came over the wood bridge from the back door to the white sand beach were any indication, the lower floors had to be pretty close to full.

After my shift was over I went for my evening swim. The beach had pretty much emptied out the later it got in the afternoon. As I swam, stroke after stroke, my mind went back to that bad place.

I was on the raft, floating out to sea, not able to stop the outward drift away from the shore and the people on the shore who were sacrificing me to the mermen, sacrificing me to save themselves from the storms that came with the summer. They were circling my raft, I could see the wake created by their strong tails under the water, and it was just a matter of moments before they flipped me off the raft and started eating my flesh…

My workout ruined, I swam back to shore.

I had trouble sleeping that night. I tossed and turned and kept waking up, it seemed like every twenty minutes. When the alarm went off at six, I turned it off and stared at the ceiling. I was tired still, mentally and physically. I lay there, staring out the window. I got out of the bed and washed my face. My eyes were red.

*I need to look good tonight. It won't kill me not to swim this morning.*

I did manage to fall asleep, deep and restful. I woke up three hours later ready to go.

Time seemed to move at a glacial pace on Friday. The minutes crawled by. By eleven the beach was wall-to-wall towels and people. I tried to stay focused on my job. I tried to keep my mind on watching the swimmers and the small kids whose mothers didn't seem to care what they were doing. But my mind kept wandering back to everything else I had going on.

I didn't know how late I would be out that night—Mobile was about an hour's drive away—and I did have to be back out on the lifeguard tower promptly at ten Saturday morning. I needed to be awake and alert and ready for anything at Dusty's. I wondered if I was being stupid, the way I had any number of times since I made up my mind to apply for the job and spend the summer at Mermaid Inn, trying to find out what happened to Zach. The police hadn't been able to find anything, nor had the private detective the Pattersons had hired after they'd given up on the Latona police department.

The PI'd even come to visit me in Corinth, waiting for me in the parking lot after swim practice, leaning against my truck while he smoked a Marlboro Red. I slowed as I walked across the parking lot. From out on the football field came the sounds of bodies colliding, grunts and groans and straining and the occasional whistle. I was carrying my bag in my right hand, my keys dangling from my left hand. He was maybe fifty and looked crumpled, disheveled. He looked like he hadn't shaved in days, hadn't seen the inside of a gym since he'd been in high school, and lived on a steady diet of drive-through hamburgers and Jack Daniel's. There was a sour smell to him. I got a good whiff of it when he asked me if I was Ricky Hackworth.

When I said I was, he offered me his hand to shake. It was calloused and warm and damp, the grip loose and limp. "The name's Gus Parr," he said, his voice raspy, like phlegm was wedged in his throat. "The Patterson family has hired me to find their son, Zach. You two were close?"

I nodded. No one had talked to me before. I wasn't sure if they would. Zach had been missing for two days before I found out. All I knew was I was getting worried. He wasn't responding to my texts, he wasn't answering my e-mails. His Facebook and Twitter accounts had gone silent. His mother had called me on the second morning, tearfully wondering if I'd heard from him or if I knew where he was. It took me several minutes to even figure out what she meant, she was struggling so hard to actually speak to me without crying or choking up. I went numb almost immediately. I'd read that before, in stories and books, how people went numb when they got bad news and had always wondered what it meant. Now I knew. It was a sick, horrible feeling, where nothing around you seems real or live and everything on the periphery of your vision goes dark, and you have to sit because your legs can't hold you anymore, and you have to really, really focus to be able to hear what's being said to you. I vaguely remember asking her if it was okay if I checked in from time to time, and hanging up when she said yes and asked me to pray for him.

I went online and read everything I could about the disappearance, which wasn't much. I waited for the police to come to me, for the FBI. I even called the police station in Latona once, to try to explain how Zach wouldn't have run away because he had no reason to run away. There was never any information that would help me—Did he leave his phone behind? Where was his laptop?—but I also knew he would have never left that car behind if he was running away.

No one ran away on foot when they had a car.

The only possible explanation was that he was dead.

I wanted to scream at his parents. *What was he doing there? Why was he even down there working for the summer with all the money you have? He didn't need to work!*

The story, as they told it to the news reporters, didn't make sense. Something had happened between him and his parents, something he hadn't been ready to share with me. He was looking forward to starting his freshman year at Alabama, he liked the idea of being only a forty-minute drive away. *I can drive down to see you pretty much any time I want to,* he'd said to me so many times I'd lost count, excitement in his voice, his blue eyes dancing. *And I can sleep over and drive back even on week nights because it's so close!* And then something changed, and he told me he'd be spending his summer lifeguarding on the Gulf Coast and wouldn't be at any of the swim camps we'd planned on going to together, asking me to not ask any questions—so I didn't because I loved him.

And here I was now, in Latona, working the same job he had, doing the same things he had done, following in his footsteps. Meeting Micah and working out at Bayside, making contact with Dane at Rocky's Auto Repair, and now getting ready to head up to Mobile to go to Dusty's, a place he'd only mentioned in passing once in an e-mail I'd reread over a thousand times.

*I went to a club called Dusty's last night. Maybe when you come down here to visit me I can take you up there. I can't describe it to you because it really has to be seen to be believed.*

There had been tinges of jealousy when he told me about Micah, when he told me about Dane. I tried to talk myself out of it, that it was just Zach. He always made friends wherever he went. He was always that way, always able to talk to anyone about anything with a quick ease I'd always envied. If he told me he loved me and they were just friends, then that was all there was and nothing else needed to be said. I knew he loved me, deep down I knew he did, but my life at home was so lonely I couldn't help but envy him his easy way with friends.

My life in the summer was the same, day in, day out. Swim. Clean pools. Swim. Clean pools. Lift weights. Watch a movie or some television with Dad or read a book before going to bed, and start the cycle over again the next day. I lived for his text messages and his e-mails. Every time my phone vibrated in my pocket while I was running the skimmer through someone's pool, I would smile because I knew it was him, because no one else ever texted me. I would check the message as soon as I could, putting the skimmer with its net full of dead bugs and leaves down and smiling at the screen of my phone, texting him back and wishing I was more eloquent so I could tell him how much I loved him, how much he meant to me, how he was my entire world. Every night as sleep came to me, my last thoughts were of him and our future together. It helped inspire me and pushed me to work harder in the pool and the weight room. I already had the scholarship offer in my pocket, but Alabama could always pull it if I underperformed in my senior season.

The loss of the scholarship would keep me from college, so it could not be allowed to happen.

The year after the summer he went to Mermaid Inn and vanished from the face of the earth had been misery, absolute misery.

The only thing that kept me going was my routine. Swim, school, swim, home, study, bed—I'm not sure when I decided to spend the summer at Mermaid Inn, trying to figure out what happened to him.

The idea had seemed crazy at first. What could I do, how could I find anything more than the police or the private eye they'd hired? But the more I thought about it, the more sense it made. I was a teenaged boy, like Zach. I was a swimmer, so was he. If I got the same job and spent the summer there, no one would think anything about a teenager, right? People would let their guard down around me, let things slip—and it was possible I could find out what exactly Zach had been doing in Latona. I decided to apply for the job. That was my roll of the dice. If I got the job, then it was meant to be. If not, I'd try to figure out a way to go on with my life and forget about Zach.

When I didn't get the job, well, that was the end of it.

But then the wheel of fate had turned again. The guy they hired quit, and they offered it to me.

Providence had intervened.

If Cecily had helped get me hired, great.

But I wasn't sure if I could trust her.

Zach had never mentioned her—or Alana, for that matter.

What if they were both lying to me?

I wondered about that up on my tower, my eyes on the water, all day Friday. Could they be trusted? Was it possible they had something to do with what happened to him, or they weren't telling me everything they knew? Maybe they didn't trust me.

His phone was trackable, surely—weren't all cell phones? Mine came with a tracking app so if I lost it, I could find it on my computer. So what happened to his phone?

What happened to *him*?

I didn't go for my evening swim once my shift on the tower was done. I went up to my room, made myself a couple of turkey sandwiches, and cleaned myself up for the evening. I didn't know what was in store for me, but Micah had told me not to worry about anything. *Just dress casually,* he'd said. *Something that shows your body off.*

I wasn't sure I had anything that fit that description. I shaved my legs, my chest, my underarms and changed the blade before shaving my face. I took a long shower, making sure to use the aftershave gel, so my freshly shaved skin didn't feel raw or burned. I put on a pair of black underwear, a worn pair of jeans Zach had always thought looked sexy on me, and a black ribbed tank top. I did some push-ups to pump up the muscles in my arms and shoulders. It was a little before eight as I went down the stairs, sipping from a bottle of water. The door to the office was closed. I shrugged to myself. Cecily knew what time Micah was picking me up. I thought she might give me some last words of warning, or suggest some kind of plan, but oh well. The way she and Alana had acted the other night...

Whatever.

I sat down on the front steps to wait for Micah.

I didn't have to wait very long. A black Explorer that had seen better days turned with a screech into the parking lot and accelerated up to the bottom of the stairs. The passenger side window went down. I could see Micah sitting behind the wheel, peering at me through mirrored sunglasses. "You ready?" he called.

I got to my feet and went down the stairs. He whistled as I opened the door and slid into the passenger seat. "Hey," I said as I buckled the seat belt.

He was grinning at me. "I like the look, that really works for you," he commented. "Understated but still sexy. What have you got on underneath the jeans? Anything?"

"Black underwear."

"Perfect." He put the car back in drive and headed down the driveway. "Do you like to dance?"

I bit my lower lip and looked out the window. "I'm not very good at it, but I can. Why?"

"Just curious." He patted my leg with his big hand. "There are lots of ways to make money at Dusty's. But the more things you can do—are willing to do—the better off you'll be."

"You still haven't told me exactly what Dusty's is," I noted as he turned back onto Shore Road, going in the opposite direction from Latona. "Other than I can make a lot of money there. Doing what exactly?"

He rested his big hand on my left leg and traced a circle on my inner thigh with his index finger. "All you have to do is look sexy, Ricky. Anything beyond that is up to you." He turned down the radio. "Dusty's is a place where a very select group of men go— it caters to them. It's a private club. Not just anyone can get in there, or even join. Even the members can't bring guests without getting them approved first."

"That sounds…weird." I kept watching the trees along the side of the road, ignoring the hand on my thigh.

"It's very exclusive."

"But we can get in?"

Micah laughed. "We're going there to work, Ricky."

"Doing what?"

"Whatever you're comfortable doing."

"Oh, that's clear," I said as sarcastically as I could.

He started laughing again. After a few minutes, he said, "These men are very important men, Ricky, and they need a place where they can go to blow off steam. Every city has a Dusty's, even if it's not called Dusty's. These men like to be surrounded by attractive men."

"It's a gay bar?"

"Kind of, but not quite." He shook his head. "You'll see."

"Am I supposed to dance or something?" Zach had been a good dancer, loose hipped with a natural sense of rhythm. He used to love to dance, told me he loved going to the dances at St. Thomas More Prep so he could shake his ass and get his groove on. I used to love watching him dance for me. He'd strip down to his underwear and bump and grind and twerk for me. I could see him dancing for money in a gay bar. He once joked that if he ever had to, he could make lots of money as a stripper.

I wasn't a good dancer. I had two left feet and no sense of rhythm at all. Every time I tried to dance, Zach would collapse in laughter, pulling me into a hug and kissing me to soothe any hurt feelings.

"You can dance if you want to. That's one of the options. But all you have to do is look good," Micah insisted. "Let the men be nice to you, that's all. Anything beyond that is up to you."

I looked out the window and didn't say anything.

The sun was setting on the other side of Mobile Bay as we headed back up toward I-10. He turned up the stereo and we didn't talk any more. I figured he thought it was just easier to let me see it for myself.

*Let the men be nice to you and look sexy. Anything beyond that is up to you.*

I swallowed.

*Oh, Zach, what were you doing last summer? Why didn't you tell me any of this? Why did you feel like you couldn't tell me what was going on with you?*

I felt like I was going to either throw up or start crying or both. I missed him so much.

After what seemed like an eternity, the truck turned into a crowded parking lot. The large two-story building had no windows. Even the door was solid, with a peephole. There wasn't a sign on the building or one for the parking lot. But I couldn't help but notice that most of the cars in the lot were expensive: Mercedes, BMW, Lexus. There was a Mobile police car parked directly across the street, and I noticed another one on the far side of the parking lot. When I mentioned them, Micah said, "I told you—the men who come here are *important.*"

I bit my lower lip. So the girls had been right about that much, anyway. The police hadn't tried too hard to find out what happened to Zach.

He was probably fed to alligators.

I wiped tears out of my eyes and forced a smile onto my face.

Micah parked the car and smiled at me. "All right, buddy, here we go." He turned off the engine. I climbed down to the gravel parking lot and took a deep breath. The night was hot, the air heavy and damp. Cars went by in both directions on the road. Out of the corner of my eye I saw movement across the street. I turned to look and saw Alana standing next to a little dark-colored Toyota. When she saw me notice her, she climbed back inside. I exhaled in relief.

I felt better knowing they were there.

"Come on." Micah waved me forward. I followed him across the parking lot. He rang the bell by the door, and a few moments later the door swung open. An enormous black man, muscle upon muscle upon muscle, his shaved head gleaming in the light from inside, practically filled the entire doorway. I could make out another door behind him, also shut, also steel. "Buddy!" he said in a deep baritone as his enormous arms went around Micah. Micah hugged him back, and the big man swung him up in the air, squeezing and shaking him. He put Micah down and looked at me. He gave a low whistle.

"You always find the prettiest boys, Micah," he growled, shaking his head. He stuck out an enormous calloused hand. "Tyrese," he said as I put my hand into his. He didn't squeeze, which was an enormous relief to me. He could probably shatter all the bones in my hand without even trying.

"Ricky."

"Come on inside. Any friend of Micah's." We stepped inside the door and it slammed shut behind us. Tyrese punched a code into the lock on the door, and it beeped and a light turned green. He swung the door open and sound blasted out, an old disco song I think I recognized as "Ring My Bell," or something like that. Zach loved old disco music and used to make me listen to it all the time.

I looked around as I followed the two of them inside. The place seemed enormous, and it looked fairly crowded. The buzz of conversation underscored the music. A cloud of smoke hung just below the ceiling. Every table was taken, men of all ages and shapes and sizes and colors gathered around. Some of them were playing poker, it looked like. There was a big open space in the center of the room, with colored lights shining. On two boxes directly opposite each other, two muscular men were dancing. Both were wearing sunglasses, the colored lights gleaming on their oiled muscles that flexed and bulged with every move they made. They both were wearing dog tags around their necks, and jeans cut off so short, they were almost as small as a Speedo. As my eyes adjusted to the dark, I saw other guys walking around carrying trays with drinks on them. They were also shirtless, wearing boxer shorts and nothing else. They were all muscular too. Every so often I noticed a shirtless guy sitting on a clothed man's lap, flirting and smiling while the clothed man's hands moved over his body.

I bit my lower lip. *Just let the men be nice to you,* I heard Micah saying.

*What did you expect it to be?*

"Take your shirt off," Micah said as he slipped his over his head, tucking it into the back of his shorts so it hung over his right butt cheek. There was no fat on his torso anywhere. His stomach rippled with muscle, and his sides were perfectly smooth as they came down into a V at the waistband of his jeans. His chest was even bigger than I'd thought it was, and he bounced both pecs at me when he noticed me looking at them. "Relax, buddy," he shouted over the music.

I hesitated for another moment before pulling my shirt off over my head. I tucked mine into the back of my pants, the way he had.

"Your body is gorgeous, Ricky," he half shouted at me, reaching over with a big hand to caress my chest. "The guys are going to love you."

"Thanks," I shouted back.

That was when I noticed framed photographs on the wall. I stepped in to get a closer look. All the pictures were of practically naked musclemen. Some were dancing on the boxes, others were dancing on the bar—

—and two guys wrestled on a mat in the center of the open space. Their bodies were coated with oil.

The one on top, his face contorted from strain and effort, was Zach.

## CHAPTER ELEVEN

Sometimes there's oil wrestling," Micah said, following my stare. "One of the reasons I asked you if you were interested in wrestling—it's all staged. I choreograph it all, with an eye to getting the guys really turned on—when they're worked up they'll spend more money." He winked at me. "And they really like the oil wrestling. The wrestlers make some serious cash here. Over a thousand a night in tips, just for getting oiled up and putting on a show for about twenty minutes. They shower the wrestlers with money...you'll see."

"Is that how you got the black eye?" I asked, unable to tear my eyes away from Zach's picture. I swallowed, trying to wrap my mind around the concept. *Zach, what were you doing here? Did you have sex with men for money? Is that why you didn't tell me what was going on with you last summer?*

I didn't want to think about it. I didn't want to believe it. It felt like my heart was being torn out of my chest all over again.

*How could you, Zach? How could you have done this to us?*

I felt like I was going to throw up.

Micah slipped his arm around my bare waist and pulled me closer until my side was pressed against his. His skin felt burning hot against mine, firm and solid. Inwardly I flinched away but managed to not let him see how revolting I found his touch. I smiled at him in what I hoped came across as shy yet flirtatious.

"Like I said, you can make some serious money here, Ricky. It's all up to you, and what you're willing to do. Obviously, the more you're willing to do, the more money you can make." He was so close I could feel his breath on my neck. "You're not a virgin, are you?"

"Of course not," I said, trying to keep my voice steady, trying not to push him away from me.

*Keep calm, keep your head. The only way you can find out what happened to Zach is to play it cool, be accepted around here. You've got to fit in.*

*No, you've got to own this place.*

"Well, that's a relief!" His hand drifted down and gripped my right butt cheek. My skin crawled, but somehow I managed to keep the smile on my face. "You probably don't have a lot of experience— you're just a kid—but some is better than none."

"I don't know—I'll have to think about *that*," I replied. "I'm not sure if I can do that…"

"Of course you can." He leaned in very close and squeezed my ass tightly. "You can make enough money this summer that you never have to lifeguard ever again."

"Who's that guy?" I pointed at the picture. "The blond? He's really hot."

I felt his body tense up, and he actually stepped away from me. "That's, um, Jack something or another. He worked here for a bit last summer."

The lie delighted me. *So, you don't want to tell me who he is? Interesting.* "He's really sexy. I wouldn't mind wrestling *him*."

"Well, that's not possible. He's not around anymore."

"Why not?" I pressed, watching as he shifted uncomfortably from foot to foot, unable to meet my eyes anymore. "I mean, if the money's so good—"

"It's not an option, okay?" His voice was flat and toneless. "Drop it."

There was a bit of menace in his voice, and when he met my eyes again, his blue eyes had gone flat.

"Jeez, man, chill out already. I was just asking." I made my voice sound light but annoyed, like I was sulking. "I thought he was hot, so sue me already, okay?"

He moved in closer to me again. "Here comes Dusty. You need to impress him, got it?"

I followed his gaze to see an enormous man working his way through the place. He was stopping and talking to people, slapping other men on the back, shaking hands with still others. There was a smile frozen into place on his big face. He was big. I don't think I've ever seen a man his size before. He had to be around six feet six, at the very least, and he was built like a professional football player. He was wearing a yellow T-shirt that had to be at least a size XXXXL. He was bald, and his big bullet-shaped head shone whenever it passed underneath a light. An enormous gold cross dangled from a gold chain around his neck, the cross bouncing on his chest as he walked. The T-shirt's sleeves looked tight enough to cut off circulation in his big beefy arms. I wondered if there was a merman under one of those sleeves. He was wearing black pleated trousers, and black wingtips on his feet. His skin was ridiculously pale, like he never got out into the sun. His eyes were narrow, and there was a thick bony ridge just above them so the eye sockets looked sunken. His mouth was wide, with thin lips over a square jaw. His nose looked squashed and flattened, like it had been broken multiple times. Diamonds on the face of the watch on his wrist glittered and sparkled whenever they caught the light. He leered at me as he approached, his eyes narrowing and moving up and down as he examined every inch of my body. I felt naked in his gaze, like he could see through my clothes, and felt myself flushing a bit in embarrassment. He smelled strongly of cologne, musky and masculine. There were thick black hairs on his huge forearms.

"Micah!" They slapped palms, and I noticed his fingernails were perfectly manicured and buffed. Several gold rings with huge diamonds glittered on his thick fingers. Micah's hand dropped from around my waist, and he moved away from me almost unnoticeably. That was when I realized I was standing directly beneath a recessed light. I was on display, and Micah had moved away so Dusty could get a good look at me. "New meat?" His voice was a deep, masculine growl that I could almost feel in my nerves. He kept leering at me, and I shifted uncomfortably as he kept staring at me. I felt vulnerable, naked. He pursed his thin lips together and whistled. His teeth were big and yellowed, with a gap between the front two top ones. "How do you always manage to find these choice cuts of sirloin?" He turned his attention away from me to Micah, who shrank a bit from his piercing gaze.

"This is Ricky, he's working in Latona for the summer. Ain't he pretty?" Micah gave me a nod. "Ricky, this is the notorious Dusty himself, lord and master of this place, and if you're lucky, your new employer."

"Pleased to meet you," he said, sticking out his meaty hand for me to shake.

"Pleasure's mine," I replied as I took his hand. My hand disappeared inside his, and I nodded with a smile as he pumped it up and down. His hand was dry and hot, and I bit my lower lip. *He could break me in half with just one hand without even trying.*

He dropped my hand and peered at me. "So, you want to make some money this summer, boy? Think you can make my customers happy?"

I kept the smile on my face and nodded. "I know I can, sir."

"The name's Dusty," he growled at me. He gestured with his other hand. "Follow me, meat."

*Meat?*

I looked at Micah, who nodded his head so slightly it was almost imperceptible. I took a deep breath and followed Dusty. The stench of smoke, both cigar and cigarette, made my eyes water and my throat close up a bit. I tried not to choke or cough as I avoided bumping into men. I was aware of people watching me, looking at me. Every so often a finger would slowly trail down the center of my back, or one would brush against my ass. It took all of my self-control not to flinch or shiver at the touch—I somehow knew a negative reaction would finish me here, get me tossed out on my ear or worse. Instead, I opened my eyes wide and smiled, hoping my facial expression looked interested or flirtatious rather than nervous, scared, and appalled. It seemed to take an eternity for us to cross through the noisy, smoky room, but it was probably only a few minutes. He stopped in front of a big steel door and pulled out a key ring. He gave me a smile that made my stomach twist and unlocked the door. He pushed it open and stood to the side so I could go into this room.

It was a claustrophobic office. Like the rest of the building there was no window, just a sense of cinder block walls closing in around me. The room was very small, and when he shut the door and moved around me, the walls seem to shrink inward even more. I struggled to keep my panic and fear down, my smile plastered on my face as he went around the big steel desk to sit in the huge chair behind it. He motioned for me to sit as he turned his head to glance at a computer screen. The enormous flat screen was turned at an angle on a corner of the desk. I could see that the screen was divided into quarters, and each quarter was a live feed from cameras I hadn't noticed. The upper left quarter showed the entry door to the club. The other three were strategically placed about the interior so there was nowhere in the main part of the club he couldn't see while seated at his desk.

While he stared at the computer, I looked around the tiny room. The walls were painted white but stained with years of accumulated nicotine. In one of the corners behind Dusty was a rusty, battered metal file cabinet, painted white. The faces of some of the unlabeled drawers were dented and scratched, etched with rust. A vent in the ceiling directly over me was blasting arctic air down. I shivered and tried to keep my teeth from chattering as I sat in a faux-leather chair facing the scarred desk. There were papers and receipts and file folders scattered over the desktop. There was also an enormous green glass ashtray, filled with crumpled cigarette butts and piled high with ash. In one of the ashtray's corners, a thoroughly chewed half cigar perched.

Dusty turned his steely gaze to me and stuck out his hand again. "Let me see your ID, kid," he said flatly.

I leaned to my left and slipped my wallet out of my back pocket. I flipped it open and removed the fake ID Micah had given me. I put it into his hand. He scrutinized it for a few moments and held it up to the light, his eyes narrowed. He snorted and handed it back. "It's fake, but it's a good fake," he said. "Micah really needs to find someone new. But it'll pass unless someone really takes a look. How old are you really, kid?"

I bit my lower lip and stuck out my chin. "Eighteen," I replied defiantly, daring him to challenge me while inside I was quaking.

"At least you're not a fucking minor," he replied. "Just always keep that fake ID on you. Not that we'll ever get raided—not with the bribes I pay in this fucking town and the dirt I have on the right fucking people—but we serve booze, and I'm not losing my liquor license for an under-aged piece of ass, no matter how hot that ass is, you understand me?" He smiled at me, but the smile didn't reach his black beady eyes.

"Yes, sir, I understand."

He seemed to like that. "So"—he leaned back in the chair, putting his hands behind his head—"what are you willing to do? How much money do you want to make?" He watched me intently.

"I—I don't know." *Stay calm,* I reminded myself. My heart was pounding so hard I couldn't believe he couldn't hear it. "I'm going to college this fall, but my scholarship doesn't cover everything, and with my swimming practice I won't be able to have a job—"

"Another swimmer—perfect." He snorted, cutting me off. He laughed. "You're not a virgin, are you?"

"No."

"Good." He barked out another laugh. "Micah knows where the money is. I should've known. Stand up."

I didn't hesitate, rising out of the chair in one fluid motion. I put my hands in my back pockets and stood there, tensing the muscles in my stomach. I could feel the blood rushing up to my face as he looked me up and down, looking for flaws, imperfections.

"You ever fucked someone?"

I nodded.

"Take your pants off."

I gaped at him. "What?"

He gestured impatiently. "Take off your goddamned pants. Are you deaf? I don't have all night. If you're just going to waste my time, you can take your ass out of here and don't come back."

I took a deep breath and kicked off my shoes. I undid my jeans and pushed them down, bending over to take them off my feet. I stood back up, putting my jeans on the chair behind me. I hooked my thumbs in the waistband of my underwear impudently. "Want me to take these off too?"

The attitude was right, because he burst into laughter. "I like your attitude, kid, you just might take to working for me after all." He shook his head. "No, you don't need to take 'em off. I can see what you have to offer. Just turn around and let me see your ass— those jeans made it look flat."

I obliged and he whistled.

"That's what I thought." I heard him get up but I didn't move, still facing the opposite wall. There were pictures on the back wall, more pictures of practically naked men with strong and muscular bodies. I glanced through them all quickly, looking for Zach. There he was, in the bottom row to the left. His head was thrown back like he was laughing. I knew that look. I'd seen it any number of times. I could hear the sound of his laughter in my head as I stared at the black-and-white image. He was wearing nothing more than a jock, and he was on his knees on a sandy beach. The water was behind him, and I realized with a start that it was Mermaid Bay. I could recognize the distant shore. I'd seen it enough times from my lifeguard tower and out the window of my room at Mermaid Inn. But it wasn't quite the same view. It was from a different spot. I focused on the picture rather than the feel of his hands cupping my buttocks, the sensation of his fingers tracing their way down the center of my back and around my shoulder blades, a slight shiver running through me as the fingertips come to rest at the waistband of my underwear. His fingers were slightly trembling. His breathing on the back of my neck grew heavier.

It was power, my power.

My body had the ability to provoke desire in other men.

*That was one of the reasons why Zach had wanted me.*

It had never occurred to me that my body had such power.

"Very nice," he said behind me in a hoarse whisper. He swallowed heavily. "So many swimmers have low, flat asses. Yours is compact, but it's shaped perfectly."

I turned around, heady with the new sense and realization of my power. I looked him directly in the eyes. "So what exactly do you have in mind for me, Mr. Dusty?"

"Can you dance?"

"I can do anything," I lied.

"But are you willing to? You're not a virgin, you said. How many men have you been with?"

*Interesting that girls—women—aren't a part of the question. But then, experience with women isn't what he's looking for in a young man, is it?*

"There's a man who will pay a lot of money for you," he went on. His breath smelled of sour liquor and stale smoke and garlic and raw onion. It was nauseating but I willed myself to ignore the stench. His lips curled up into a predatory smile. I didn't flinch, didn't blink, but kept looking directly into his ratlike eyes. "He likes them tall and young and strong with the endurance of swimmers."

*Zach,* I thought. *Like Zach.*

He cradled the front of my underwear and I reacted. His eyes narrowed and expanded again. He laughed. "Oh yes, he'll like very much." He moved back around the desk and sat again. "You're going to make us both a lot of money this summer, Ricky, my boy. It all depends on what you're willing to do for it."

I raised my chin. I remained standing. "I'm tired of being poor."

"Then stick with me, kid, and you won't have to worry about money again," he replied. He opened one of the drawers of the file cabinet. He riffled through it and tossed me a pair of skimpy bright red Lycra swim trunks. "Put those on."

I didn't turn around. I slipped my underwear down and put my feet through the leg holes of the trunks. I slid them slowly and carefully up my legs, aware the whole time of his eyes burning through my skin. I took my time, making sure the muscles in my arms and legs contracted and flexed as I worked the suit on, snapping it in the back. It was cut low, so the deep lines leading from the top of my pelvic bone down into my groin stood out. It barely covered me in the back. *You can do this,* I reminded myself, *you have to— this is the only way you can find out what happened to Zach.*

But where was I going to keep my phone? There was nowhere I could hide it, no way I could keep it on me. I couldn't call or text for help…

Maybe this was how Zach got separated from his? If something happened to him when he was just wearing a bikini…

I closed my eyes and willed myself to not think about him being killed, what his last moments must have been like.

*This is why you're here, that is why you're doing this.*

I opened my eyes.

And for a moment I wondered what Zach had felt like when he'd stood here in front of Dusty, this dirty, filthy, disgusting pig of a man. I wondered why he'd been willing to do this for money. How bad had that fight with his parents been? Surely he must have known they would have come around, he was their only child, it must have just been the shock of telling them. I couldn't imagine, even now, how his parents could have turned so vehemently against him. I remembered the broken voice of his mother on the phone when she'd asked me if I'd heard from him.

Zach might not have seen this as debasement.

Zach had never been shy about his body.

Maybe he'd sensed, as I had, the power his body gave him over men like Dusty and had just embraced it.

*Why didn't you tell me any of this? Why didn't you tell me what you were going through?*

"Tonight, you'll dance," Dusty went on. "You keep your tips, of course, and you get a base pay of a hundred bucks for the night. Make the customers happy and you'll make lots of money." He held up his smartphone and quickly snapped several pictures of me. "I'm going to get in touch with the man who's going to be your primary source of income for the summer—he'll want pictures, of course, but once he sees them…" He licked his lips. "Now turn around and show me your ass again." I did as directed. He picked up the phone on his desk and pressed a button as I turned around to face him again. "Get in here. We've got some new meat you need to show the ropes."

I picked up my clothes and folded them neatly. The room was silent other than his heavy breathing. I was aware that he was watching me, drinking in every inch of my body. I was wondering if one of my duties would be satisfying him, when I heard the door open.

I turned to look and found myself facing Dane.

He started when he saw me, and his jaw dropped a bit. He quickly shut his mouth. All he was wearing was a pair of black work boots and a Tarzan-like loincloth. He smirked. "Micah got you here." It was a statement, not a question. "Come with me."

I followed him out of the office back into the main room. I ignored the looks we were getting. There was a tattoo of wings across his lower back, just above where the string of his loincloth circled his body. He was tanned all over. He stopped in front of another door, which he pushed open. It was a smaller-scale locker room, long and narrow with a bench in the center between the rows of rusty lockers pushed against the walls. There was a full-length mirror mounted on the wall in the back. The upper right-hand corner was broken off. He spun a combination lock on one of the lockers and pulled it open. "You'll need to bring your own lock," he said. "You can keep your stuff in mine tonight."

I placed my clothes on top of his. He was leaning against the lockers, arms folded in front of him, muscles bulging. "Thanks."

"I might have known Micah would get to you," he said, shaking his head from side to side so his thick hair floated. "It's the damned gym. He has better access."

I closed the locker door. "Is this what you meant about making money?" I asked, leaning against the closed locker, mimicking his pose with my arms folded. I bounced my pecs at him. "Is that what that other lifeguard did? The one who went missing? Do I need to be careful around here?"

"Don't bring him up around here if you know what's good for you," he hissed through his clenched teeth. "He wasn't—he wasn't smart, if you know what I mean. I tried to warn him. And you need to be careful too."

"What do you mean?"

"Look, the men who come here—you need to understand something." He leaned in, lowering his voice to a whisper. "The men who come here are powerful. They come here because they have money and power and a lot to lose if anyone ever finds out about this place. They've got wives, families. They're the power structure of this city, and any number of other cities on the coast around here. And if you try to cause any trouble for them, well"— he snapped his fingers—"they'll make you disappear. Just like that. And they can get away with it."

"Is that what happened to him? They made him disappear?"

"I don't know what happened to him," he insisted. "He just vanished one day. All Dusty would say about it was warn us about trying anything with the clients. *You're paid very well to keep your goddamned mouths shut, so keep that in mind and you'll make some nice money and you won't vanish.* It sounded pretty clear to me." He put his hands on my chest. "And you're going to wind up with the same guy he did, you know. He likes a specific type, and you're it." He shook his head. "You need to be fucking careful, you understand? You need to be really, really careful."

"Who is this guy?"

He shook his head again and gave me a sad smile. "Roger. Roger Rossitter." He bit his lower lip. "Always make sure when you go out to his place that someone knows where you are—someone who's not from around here. Roger owns Latona, Ricky. He owns it lock, stock, and barrel. And never forget they can make you just disappear. Just keep your nose clean and don't make the same mistakes he did. Now let's go make some money."

I followed him back out into the main room. The two guys dancing on the boxes jumped down when we walked out into the center area. I jumped up on one and just stood there for a moment. No one was paying attention to us. The men at the table were talking and laughing and smoking and drinking. Here and there a shirtless younger man was perched on a lap. The two dancers we'd replaced began making their way around the room. I started moving awkwardly. A man came up and pinched my nipples and placed a twenty-dollar bill into the elastic waistband of my trunks. I smiled at him and said thank you. I saw Micah in a darkened corner. He had both arms up, his huge muscles flexed as a man in a suit groped the muscles, occasionally pressing his mouth to them.

I began to lose track of time. The smoke, the noise, the hands of the men touching me, their lips pressing against my flat stomach, the almost furtive slipping of a bill into my trunks. I saw Dane put his money into his sock, and I did the same thing. It didn't seem to matter that I really couldn't dance. All that mattered was the visual, my bare skin, the skimpy bathing suit, the muscles moving beneath my skin, the raised veins on my muscles. Sometimes a man would ask me to pose, to flex a particular muscle, and I would as he stroked the muscle with light fingertips before moving away, after paying, always paying. No one ever came up, no one touched, no one spoke, without paying for the privilege afterward.

*My body is power, it is my currency.*

And Zach, I could see how he would have felt, reacted to this. He loved his body, was proud of it. He never raced or practiced in anything other than a bikini cut. Even when others were moving to longer shorts or even tights that encased the entire leg, Zach proudly climbed up onto the block before the starting gun in his skimpy little Speedo with his entire body on complete display. *I've worked really hard for my body, so why not show it off and be proud of it? I'm not ashamed of it. And people want to see it.*

And I could see the attraction, the allure, the pull of destiny and desire and lust and pride that came from having strangers stare at you, appreciating your physical beauty so much that they would give you money to just touch it, for you to show it off to them. And then Micah was in front of me, a big smile on his face, standing there shirtless with his hands on his hips, his shorts hanging down so low I could see his pubic hair, and he was so clearly not wearing anything underneath, and I could see the look in his blue eyes, the same look the others had as he smiled and placed a twenty-dollar bill into my trunks.

He said something I couldn't hear over the noise, so I leaned down and he whispered into my ear. "I'm going to be gone for a little while but don't worry, I'm just going to go make some money but I'll be here to drive you back home, no worries, I won't strand you up here." And the whole time he was whispering in my ear, his big hands were cupping my butt cheeks, and I realized I was flexing the muscles, making them harder in his hands, and I was amazed, amazed at how easily this was all coming to me.

*Did it come easy for you, Zach? But why were you here in the first place?*

The other dancers came back, and it was time for me to walk around the club, sitting on laps, flirting, getting money out of men, older men who stank of power and money and privilege. I saw it as a game, and I smiled at them and flirted and lied. They were the same people my dad worked for, the ones who forgot to pay and dismissed his concerns and treated him like he was beneath their notice, the same way their children treated me like I was something they'd scrape from the bottom of their shoes, making fun of my clothes and my shyness and my dad's lack of money and our sad, pitiful little house with the rusty tin roof, that was always too hot in the summer and too cold in the winter. I hated these men with the same burning hatred I felt for their compatriots back in Corinth, rich and spoiled and so unaware of the privilege and gifts their money gave them, so unaware of what it was like to have to deal with them and to not be one of them. The hatred burned in me so brightly, that I felt it glowing out of my eyes, and it made me smile brighter and utter the flirtatious words I'd never been able to say before, that I would have never imagined myself able to say, pouring out of my mouth like an elixir, a magical potion designed to get them to give me money.

I loved having this power over them, the power of youth and beauty and desire. And then I got back up on the box and danced some more, my socks now full of damp and sweaty money, so much of it that I was almost afraid to count it, and the night went on, and everything began to blur together, the faces and the hands and the money, the money always changing hands, coming forward, and the smoke and the smell and the warm sweaty hands, the damp bills.

It was power, and I embraced it and loved it.

## CHAPTER TWELVE

I didn't swim Saturday morning.

I was exhausted when my phone went off at six. I turned it off and reset it for nine.

It had been sometime after four when Micah dropped me off at Mermaid Inn. The building was dark, other than some night-lights here and there should the guests get up and wander in the middle of the night. I could hear the waves kissing the shore behind. The sky was cloudless, purplish black with stars glittering like diamonds. I was tired physically but my mind was jumping, alive, awake, and aware.

I'd never felt more alive.

I reeked of sweat and smoke. I felt like my skin was covered with greasy fingerprints. But the money, the money! There was so much of it, all of it grubby and damp and soaked in sweat and stink, but I counted almost a thousand dollars.

A thousand dollars! For nothing more than standing on a box, smiling at men, and letting them touch me.

And pretending I liked it. Pretending that I was interested, that I wanted them to do more to me than fondle me and stroke my muscles and tweak my nipples. That was my power, and I relished it, reveled in it.

*No wonder Zach didn't tell me about this—it's intoxicating to know the power I have over other men.*

I showered before getting in my bed. I was desperate to get the stink of the club off me. Before going to bed I opened my window and put the smoky clothes out on the roof to air out. I didn't want that stink in my room all night. Shivering a bit as I pulled the blankets up over me, I drifted down into sleep almost the minute my head hit the pillow.

I didn't dream. I thought I might, but the physical exhaustion overpowered my brain.

At nine I dragged myself out of the bed. I got my clothes back in from the roof. They didn't stink anymore and the sweat had dried them stiff. I took another long, hot shower, scrubbing my skin until it was raw. My nipples were a bit sore from being pinched and tweaked and pulled all night. I got dressed, made a big breakfast, went down the stairs, and climbed back up into my tower. I was tired, so tired, and afraid I'd fall asleep behind my sunglasses, having to sometimes pinch myself to be certain I wasn't asleep and dreaming. Thoughts of money danced through my head. A thousand dollars per night, two or three nights a week, and I would have so much money I wouldn't know what to do with it all by the end of the summer.

The waves washed ashore. The water was like glass and the sun's reflection was glaring, hurting my tired eyes even behind the sunglasses. More and more people came to the beach, spreading towels and blankets, blaring portable stereos. My mind darted around.

I was so close, so close to finding out what happened to Zach I could hardly stand it.

*But what if finding out means you won't make any more of the money?*

I dismissed that contemptible thought.

There were other ways I could make money.

I pulled the slip of paper from my wallet. *He'll pay you a thousand dollars, less my cut, of course, for just a few hours,* I heard Dusty saying to me again after he'd gotten me down from the box, earning an angry glare from the rat-looking man who'd been about to give me a grope and some cash. *It's easy for you, you don't even have to leave town. If he likes you, it may even be more than once a week. He'll pay it to me, and I'll give you your share. Eight hundred bucks, boy, eight hundred bucks for just a couple of hours. Where else you gonna get that kind of money for that little time?*

I looked at the name.

Roger Rossitter.

I heard Dane's voice again in my head. *Always make sure someone not from Latona knows where you are. He owns the town, lock, stock, and barrel, and no one else can be trusted.*

When I'd walked out with Micah I didn't see the girls anywhere, but it was late.

The entire way back to Latona, Micah's hand had rested on my leg. When he dropped me off, the last words he'd said to me were *I told you I could help you make some money this summer, didn't I? Leave it to old Micah. I'll take care of you, Ricky.*

Like he took care of Zach?

The waves lapped against the shoreline as the sun kept rising in the sky. The heat and humidity, the swampiness of the sea air, the damp breeze blowing in from the water all combined to lull me into an almost dreamlike stupor. Voices swirled in my head, images from last night of hands groping at me, Zach smiling at the camera with his body glistening with oil, the stink of the stale smoke and sour liquor, the lusty leers and dirty smiles. I closed my eyes and warded off sleep. I pulled out my phone and searched again for information about Roger Rossitter. There was hardly anything, like the last time I'd looked. But now, the articles about paying for the library and political donations and all the other things he'd done for Latona sounded ominous and threatening. There was a pattern of buying influence and power. Who would question such a charitable man, who did so much for his community? The last of a long line of a wealthy family who'd built the town, employed people, and tossed money around like there was an endless supply, doing good things like paying for libraries and giving money to health clinics and so on?

Who'd believe he was a vicious murderer?

Yet somehow I just knew this was the right one, the man who had the answers I needed. I knew it in my heart. He was the last person to see Zach alive. He had done it, made him vanish, and somehow I had to make him pay for it.

I didn't see Cecily much. She came out with a turkey sandwich for me around noon and a bottle of water. She tried to get information out of me about my night at Dusty's, but I brushed her questions off, finally telling her I was too tired and I would talk to her about it later. The beach was crowded, and while I could see she was reluctant to let it go, the Inn's guests were everywhere and the last thing she needed was for them to hear anything we said to each other.

I couldn't help but wonder what had happened to Zach's laptop. Someone with a master key could have taken it.

*You can't trust anyone in Latona. He owns everyone.*

Cecily—or Joe? What about Alana?

They'd tried to warn me about Micah and Dane, both. Could I trust Dane?

It was around four when the message I was waiting for beeped into my phone.

*I'll pick you up at the bottom of the driveway at eight. Don't be late. RR*

He liked my pictures, he liked me, and this meant pay for play.

There was no doubt in my mind that this was what had happened to Zach.

And probably all of the others too.

At six, I climbed down from the tower and went up to my room. I washed my face and lay back down on the bed after getting some coffee started. Even though I was physically and emotionally exhausted, I was also sort of wired. This was it. This was everything I had thought about and planned ever since Zach's parents had called me, wondering if I'd heard from him, the hope in their voices almost breaking my heart. I packed my shoulder bag and drank coffee. I showered and checked my body. There was no stubble yet on my legs, my chest, my underarms. I put on a pair of khaki shorts and a black tank top. At seven fifty I went down the stairs with my bag slung over my shoulder, a bottle of water in my hands. As I went out the front door, I remembered everything I'd read about Zach's disappearance.

*He went out the front door at eight to walk into town. No one ever saw him again.*

History was repeating itself.

But I would have my phone with me, and it would be charged.

I walked down the slope of the parking lot, taking the occasional swig from the bottle. The sun was setting in the west, the blue of the sky darkening to the purple of night. It was getting cooler. It was still hot, and the warm damp still hung in the air like a woolen blanket taken out of the dryer twenty minutes too soon. Just like that first day, but nothing like it. I stood there at the bottom of the parking lot, waiting.

Just as the minute hand on my watch moved and it was eight, a dark green convertible sports car roared around the curve from the left. It screeched up to the parking lot and the passenger window went down. "Get in," a male voice said.

I opened the door and slid into the passenger seat. It was soft leather, like butter caressing my skin. He made a U-turn and revved the engine back in the direction he'd come from.

He smelled of expensive cologne. He was wearing a baseball cap pulled low on his forehead, and his eyes were hidden behind mirrored sunglasses. His legs looked tanned and muscular, covered with dark curly hairs as were his tanned forearms. He was wearing a polo style shirt, dark green to match the car, and khaki shorts. Classical music came out of the stereo speakers. About a half mile up the road he turned left, into a driveway. It curved through towering pine trees and came out in front of a small two-story house, raised up on pilings about six feet off the ground, with a white sandy beach below. There was a deck around the first floor, and behind the house a pier ran out into the bay. He parked and turned to me. "Welcome." He smiled at me, his thin lips parting and showing even white teeth, perfectly shaped and perfectly aligned. His jaw was strong and square, with a slight cleft in the center of his pointed chin. His thinning dark hair was strewn with white hairs.

"Thank you," I said. It was the first time I'd spoken since I'd gotten into the car. I opened the door and stood, stretching. I was still tired, but the coffee had wired me some. I shut the car door and waited for him.

He was short, but he was stocky and muscular. He walked around the car and stood in front of me, so close I could feel his breath on my chest. He reached out and grabbed my biceps with his hands. They were warm. He squeezed, and his breath was coming harder. "You're exactly what I need," he said in a hoarse whisper.

*Power. My body is power.*

He took me by the hand and led me up the wooden steps to the deck. Wind chimes gently sang in the breeze. Louvered windows were open all around the lower floor of the house. He unlocked the door and held it aside so I could walk in. There was an outer patio, a Florida room, with cushioned wicker rocking chairs and a cushioned wicker couch. In one of the corners stained-glass chimes hung, moving slightly in the wind and ringing out their song. He unlocked the inner door and led me inside. The entire first floor was one enormous room, with a kitchenette in one corner and a wet bar. The floor was checkerboard tile, alternating black and white. There was the steady humming of air conditioning.

"Make yourself comfortable," he said, gesturing to the living room. "Can I get you something to drink? What's your poison?"

"I'm fine with water," I replied. I sat on the couch, slouching so my legs were stretched out in front of me, crossed at the ankles. I watched as he made himself a drink—bourbon on the rocks. He walked over and sat beside me.

"You're exactly what I need," he said, placing a hand on my leg and tracing a circle with his index finger on my inner thigh.

I smiled up at him and could hear Dane's voice in my head. *They don't really care about the sex that much. They're really just looking for companionship, someone to listen to them and make a fuss over them. The talking—that's most of the night. The sex is over before you even know it, and all you really have to do is make them think they're the best lover you've ever had.*

His breath was faster, harder.

His fingers were creeping closer to the bottom of my shorts.

I stood and pulled my shirt over my head in one fluid motion. I got down onto my knees in front of him and took both of his hands in mine and placed them on my chest.

"I'm not the first boy you've brought here," I said, keeping my voice low and what I hoped was seductive.

"No." He leaned forward, and I could smell his breath, wintergreen mouthwash over something slightly more fetid and sour. "But you're the best one. You're exactly what I love, what turns me on. Tall and lean and strong and powerful and blond, your skin is so soft and smooth." His breathing was coming faster with each word, and I wondered if he could hear the loud thump of my own rapid heartbeat.

But if he could, he would assume it was excitement.

It was, but not the kind he would think.

"Let's go up to the bedroom," he said hoarsely, getting to his feet and taking me by the hand. I stood and followed him up the metal spiral staircase to the upper floor, which like the lower one was simply one enormous room with a bed in the center. He led me to the bed and pushed me down onto it gently. He climbed on top of me, pulling his own shirt over his head. His chest was covered with thick black hair, but in the center of his chest it had turned white. He bent down and pressed his moist lips against my throat and began kissing me, the tip of his tongue darting out to lick and taste my skin every so often. I lay there, unmoving, staring at the terracotta ceiling, which was painted a dark blue with stars. I focused on the ceiling fan as his mouth moved down my torso.

Suddenly he sat up again.

He smiled down at me. "Let me go to the bathroom and get ready. I won't be a minute. Get undressed while I'm in there."

It wasn't a request.

That was when I noticed the merman tattooed on his upper arm.

Like Micah's. Like Dane's.

He went around the corner into an area marked off by opaque glass bricks, and I stood up. I took off my shorts and underwear and neatly folded them, putting them on the nightstand. I made sure the pocket with my phone in it was on the top, in case I needed it.

*Who are you kidding? You know you're going to need it.*

I could hear water running in the bathroom. I sat back down on the edge of the bed.

He was singing to himself in the bathroom.

I opened the top drawer of the nightstand.

There were condoms scattered about inside, along with several other items. Some rings, a couple of cell phones, some other assorted jewelry.

One of the phones was a white iPhone.

*There are millions of those in the world, Ricky.*

Being careful not to touch it, I used a pen to flip it over to the back.

Engraved on the back were the words *Happy Birthday Zach— Love, Mom and Dad.*

I'd seen it before.

I heard Zach's voice in my head again, saying *Mom and Dad bought me a new phone for my birthday, so I'm giving you my old one. I've reset it back to factory settings, and all you have to do is get a new SIM card and presto! You have a smartphone.*

I licked my lower lip.

No one had ever found Zach's phone because it had been here the whole time.

The last person to see Zach was his killer.

He was still singing in the bathroom, the water was still running.

I used the pen to pick up one of the rings. It was a Latona High class ring, two years old. I looked on the inside.

*ABC* was engraved on the inside.

*Augustin Benjamin Correro.*

My heart started beating just a little bit faster. That name was on my spreadsheet.

*He'd disappeared two years ago.*

The blood was pounding in my ears.

I reached for my phone.

I opened the camera app and took a picture of the phone and the engraving. I took another of the ring, making sure I got the engraving on the inside.

The water was still running in the bathroom.

I didn't know how much time I had.

I typed a text out as quickly as I could with my fingers shaking.

*Here's the evidence you need.*

I attached both images to the text and hit the send button.

I stood and carefully slid the drawer closed again.

My phone vibrated. *Get out of there, we're on our way,* the text read.

I knew it was the smart thing to do. But somehow, I couldn't do it.

I had to know.

I had to ask.

I walked across the hardwood floor, my feet not making a sound.

I came around the corner of the glass blocks. Roger had his back to me. There were love handles at his waist, and he was naked, a bikini tan line making his slightly sagging buttocks bright white against the tan, dark hairs in the crevice.

"You killed them all, didn't you?" I said, just loud enough to be heard over the water.

"What?" Roger reached down and turned off the spigots. The water stopped. There was a gurgling sound as the shower floor drained. He reached for a towel, wrapping it around his waist before turning around. He had a strange look on his face. "What did you just say?"

"I said, you killed them all, didn't you?"

"What are you talking about?" He grabbed another towel and started wiping the beads of water off his chest. "Maybe you'd better just go."

"I have to know." I crossed my arms, leaned against the glass-block wall. Every instinct in my body was screaming for me to run, to get the hell out of there—but I couldn't. I couldn't go without asking, without getting the answers. "Why? Why did you kill them all?"

"Maybe you'd better leave." Roger whipped the towel over his head, started rubbing it across his back. His voice sounded placid, calm. He *knew* what I was asking him, I could see it in his face, hear it in his voice.

"And you're going to kill me," I went on casually, like we were just talking about the weather. "What I don't understand is why. That's all I want, Roger. Please."

Roger relaxed and barked out a laugh. "I think you need to go." He stepped closer and gave me a little push. "And keep going. Pack up your shit back at the Inn and get the fuck out of this town because I will destroy you."

I took a step backward. "Zach was my *boyfriend*"—I took another step back—"and you killed him. Why? Why would you do such a thing?"

He smiled. "I get off on it," he whispered. "I love watching the light go out in their eyes. And Zach had such *pretty* eyes."

*Come on, come on,* I thought, wondering what was taking so long, and the fear started to rise inside of me. His eyes—

*His eyes.*

There was madness there.

And then he was on me. It happened so fast I didn't see it coming, didn't have time to react. We fell backward to the floor, all the breath forced out of my lungs as he landed on top of me, my head bouncing off the wooden floor and stars dancing in front of my eyes, and then his hands were around my throat. I grabbed his wrists but he was too strong, I was too dizzy and confused and couldn't breathe, couldn't get enough air into my lungs and everything started getting fuzzy and—

—and then he wasn't there anymore and I could breathe again. Gasping, I rolled over to my side and looked up as I greedily sucked air in. I was vaguely aware he was being handcuffed, and someone was helping me up to my feet. I put my hand against the wall. My throat hurt, my head was throbbing from where it hit the floor.

"Are you all right?" I knew the voice, even through the weird roaring in my ears. It was Special Agent Brady Byrnes.

"I—I think so," I rasped out.

"Come on," he said, leading me by the arm out to the deck behind the house. "What were you thinking? I told you to get out."

I leaned over the railing, staring down at the black water of the bay, the waves coming in to the shore. "I know. I…I had to know. I had to ask him why."

He didn't say anything for a moment. We stood there on the deck, no sound other than the breaking waves beneath us. Finally he placed his hand on my shoulder and said softly, "He's going away for a very long time, Ricky. We may never know why he did it, why he killed all those boys. But you did very good work. You ever consider a career with the FBI?"

I shook my head. The roaring was dying down, and my throat was still sore. "No." I exhaled. "This was *personal.* I don't know. I just want to go to college and swim."

"You have plenty of time to decide," he replied. He squeezed my shoulder with his hand. "You were very brave, Ricky. Not everyone could have pulled this off, you know. We made the right choice in asking you to do this." He let go. "You stay out here, I'm going to go check on things inside. You're going to have to give a statement—I'll send someone out."

I nodded and heard his footsteps cross the gallery and go back inside. I covered my face with my hands, rubbing my eyes.

It was over, at long last.

I pulled out my phone and sent my dad a brief text message: *It's over, Dad.*

I stared out at the bay, the blackness of the water. Overhead the stars blinked in a purplish-black sky.

It was over.

"Rest in peace, Zach," I whispered. "I love you."

The waves continued to roll in beneath me.

# About the Author

Greg Herren is a New Orleans-based author and editor. He is a co-founder of the Saints and Sinners Literary Festival, which takes place in New Orleans every May. He is the author of twenty novels, including the Lambda Literary Award winning *Murder in the Rue Chartres*, called by the *New Orleans Times-Picayune* "the most honest depiction of life in post-Katrina New Orleans published thus far." He co-edited *Love, Bourbon Street: Reflections on New Orleans*, which also won the Lambda Literary Award. His young adult novel *Sleeping Angel* won the Moonbeam Gold Medal for Excellence in Young Adult Mystery/Horror. He has published over fifty short stories in markets as varied as *Ellery Queen's Mystery Magazine* to the critically acclaimed anthology *New Orleans Noir* to various websites, literary magazines, and anthologies. His erotica anthology *FRATSEX* is the all time best selling title for Insightoutbooks. He has worked as an editor for Bella Books, Harrington Park Press, and now Bold Strokes Books.

A long-time resident of New Orleans, Greg was a fitness columnist and book reviewer for Window Media for over four years, publishing in the LGBT newspapers *IMPACT News*, *Southern Voice*, and *Houston Voice*. He served a term on the Board of Directors for the National Stonewall Democrats, and served on the founding committee of the Louisiana Stonewall Democrats. He is currently employed as a public health researcher for the NO/AIDS Task Force, and is serving a term on the board of the Mystery Writers of America.

# Soliloquy Titles From Bold Strokes Books

**Searching for Grace** by Juliann Rich. First it's a rumor. Then it's a fact. And then it's on. (978-1-62639-196-3)

**Dark Tide** by Greg Herren. A summer working as a lifeguard at a hotel on the Gulf Coast seems like a dream job...until Ricky Hackworth realizes the town is shielding some very dark—and deadly—secrets. (978-1-62639-197-0)

**Everything Changes** by Samantha Hale. Raven Walker's world is turned upside down the moment Morgan O'Shea walks into her life. (978-1-62639-303-5)

**Tristant and Elijah** by Jennifer Lavoie. After Elijah finds a scandalous letter belonging to Tristant's great uncle, the boys set out to discover the secret Uncle Glenn kept hidden his entire life and end up discovering who they are in the process. (978-1-62639-075-1)

**Caught in the Crossfire** by Juliann Rich. Two boys at Bible camp; one forbidden love. (978-1-62639-070-6)

**Remember Me** by Melanie Batchelor. After a tragic event occurs, teenager Jamie Richards is left questioning the identity of the girl she loved, Erica Sinclair. (978-1-62639-184-0)

**Frenemy of the People** by Nora Olsen. Clarissa and Lexie have despised each other as long as they can remember, but when they both find themselves helping an unlikely contender for homecoming queen, they are catapulted into an unexpected romance. (978-1-62639-063-8)

**The Balance** by Neal Wooten. Love and survival come together in the distant future as Piri and Niko face off against the worst factions of mankind's evolution. (978-1-62639-055-3)

**The Unwanted** by Jeffrey Ricker. Jamie Thomas is plunged into danger when he discovers his mother is an Amazon who needs his help to save the tribe from a vengeful god. (978-1-62639-048-5)

**Because of Her** by KE Payne. When Tabby Morton is forced to move to London, she's convinced her life will never be the same again. But the beautiful and intriguing Eden Palmer is about to show her that this time, change is most definitely for the better. (978-1-62639-049-2)

**Asher's Fault** by Elizabeth Wheeler. Fourteen-year-old Asher Price sees the world in black and white, much like the photos he takes, but when his little brother drowns at the same moment Asher experiences his first same-sex kiss, he can no longer hide behind the lens of his camera and eventually discovers he isn't the only one with a secret. (978-1-60282-982-4)

**The Seventh Pleiade** by Andrew J. Peters. When Atlantis is besieged by violent storms, tremors, and a barbarian army, it will be up to a young gay prince to find a way for the kingdom's survival. (978-1-60282-960-2)

**The Missing Juliet: A Fisher Key Adventure** by Sam Cameron. A teenage detective and her friends search for a kidnapped Hollywood star in the Florida Keys. (978-1-60282-959-6)

**Meeting Chance** by Jennifer Lavoie. When man's best friend turns on Aaron Cassidy, the teen keeps his distance until fate puts Chance in his hands. (978-1-60282-952-7)

**Lake Thirteen** by Greg Herren. A visit to an old cemetery seems like fun to a group of five teenagers, who soon learn that sometimes it's best to leave old ghosts alone. (978-1-60282-894-0)

**The Road to Her** by KE Payne. Sparks fly when actress Holly Croft, star of UK soap *Portobello Road*, meets her new on-screen love interest, the enigmatic and sexy Elise Manford. (978-1-60282-887-2)

**Swans and Klons** by Nora Olsen. In a future world where there are no males, sixteen-year-old Rubric and her girlfriend Salmon Jo must fight to survive when everything they believed in turns out to be a lie. (978-1-60282-874-2)

**Kings of Ruin** by Sam Cameron. High school student Danny Kelly and loner Kevin Clark must team up to defeat a top-secret alien intelligence that likes to wreak havoc with fiery car, truck, and train accidents. (978-1-60282-864-3)

**Wonderland** by David-Matthew Barnes. After her mother's sudden death, Destiny Moore is sent to live with her two gay uncles on Avalon Cove, a mysterious island on which she uncovers a secret place called Wonderland, where love and magic prove to be real. (978-1-60282-788-2)

**Another 365 Days** by KE Payne. Clemmie Atkins is back, and her life is more complicated than ever! Still madly in love with her girlfriend, Clemmie suddenly finds her life turned upside down with distractions, confessions, and the return of a familiar face... (978-1-60282-775-2)

**The Secret of Othello** by Sam Cameron. Florida teen detectives Steven and Denny risk their lives to search for a sunken NASA satellite—but under the waves, no one can hear you scream… (978-1-60282-742-4)

**Andy Squared** by Jennifer Lavoie. Andrew never thought anyone could come between him and his twin sister, Andrea…until Ryder rode into town. (978-1-60282-743-1)

**Sara** by Greg Herren. A mysterious and beautiful new student at Southern Heights High School stirs things up when students start dying. (978-1-60282-674-8)

**OMGqueer** edited by Radclyffe and Katherine E. Lynch, PhD. Through stories imagined and told by youth across America, this anthology provides a snapshot of queerness at the dawn of the new millennium. (978-1-60282-682-3)

**Street Dreams** by Tama Wise. Tyson Rua has more than his fair share of problems growing up in New Zealand—he's gay, he's falling in love, and he's run afoul of the local hip-hop crew leader just as he's trying to make it as a graffiti artist. (978-1-60282-650-2)

**me@you.com** by KE Payne. Is it possible to fall in love with someone you've never met? Imogen Summers thinks so because it's happened to her. (978-1-60282-592-5)

**Swimming to Chicago** by David-Matthew Barnes. As the lives of the adults around them unravel, high school students Alex and Robby form an unbreakable bond, vowing to do anything to stay together—even if it means leaving everything behind. (978-1-60282-572-7)

**365 Days** by KE Payne. Life sucks when you're seventeen years old and confused about your sexuality, and the girl of your dreams doesn't even know you exist. Then in walks sexy new emo girl, Hannah Harrison. Clemmie Atkins has exactly 365 days to discover herself, and she's going to have a blast doing it! (978-1-60282-540-6)

**Timothy** by Greg Herren. *Timothy* is a romantic suspense thriller from award-winning mystery writer Greg Herren set in the fabulous Hamptons. (978-1-60282-760-8)